GOING ALL THE WAY

SEAN O'LEARY

Copyright (C) 2021 Sean O'Leary

Layout design and Copyright (C) 2021 by Next Chapter

Published 2021 by Next Chapter

Edited by Brice Fallon

Cover art by Cover Mint

This book is a work of fiction. Names, characters, places, and incidents are the product of the author's imagination or are used fictitiously. Any resemblance to actual events, locales, or persons, living or dead, is purely coincidental.

All rights reserved. No part of this book may be reproduced or transmitted in any form or by any means, electronic or mechanical, including photocopying, recording, or by any information storage and retrieval system, without the author's permission.

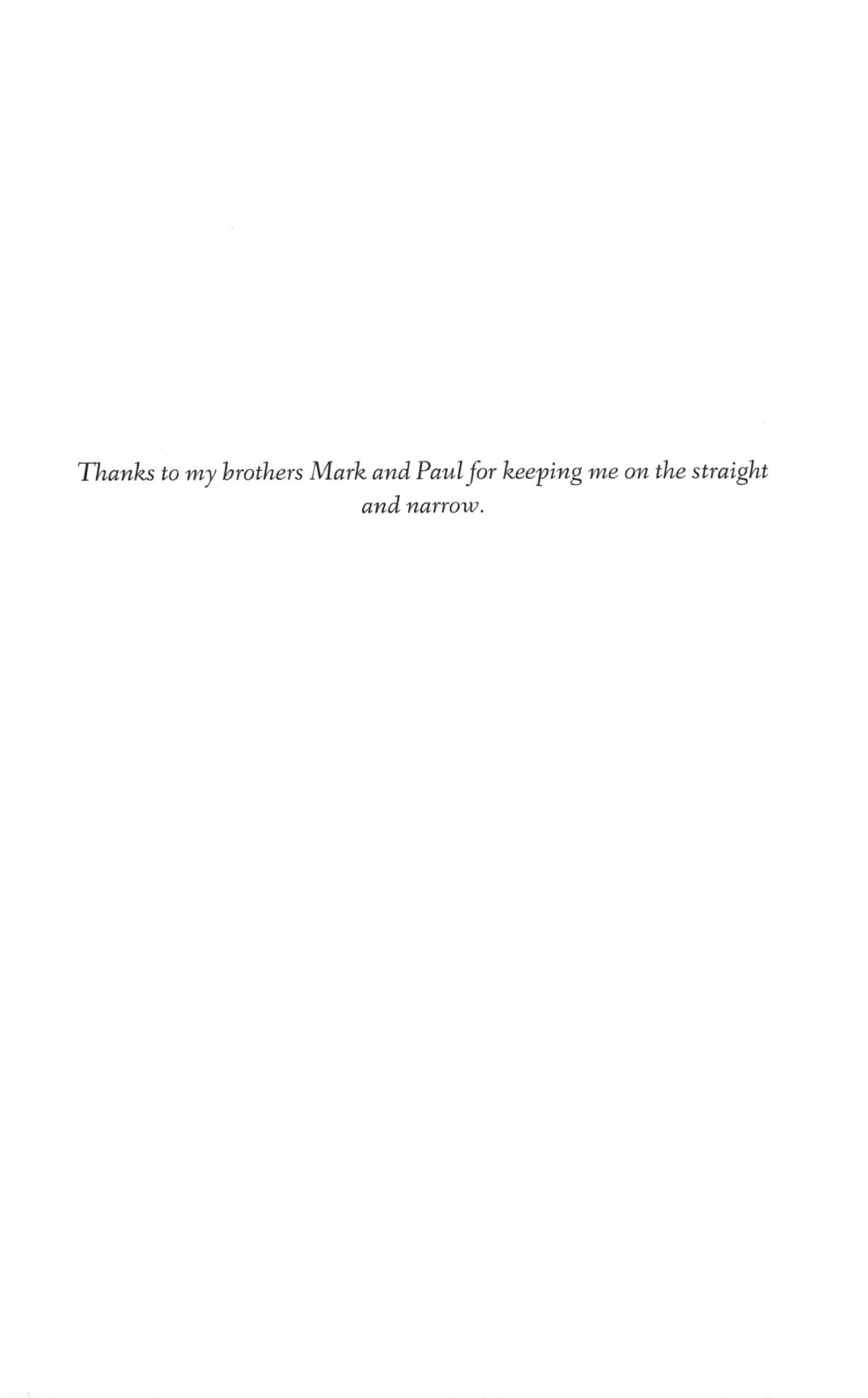

Thanks to my brothers Mark and Paul for keeping me on the straight and narrow.

In writing, I'm totally anti-plans of any kind. All my attempts to plot and plan novels have come to grief, and in expensive ways...
    Peter Temple

CHAPTER ONE

The night manager stands in the doorway of the motel on Darlinghurst Road. Lights a cigarette. The bloodstained sheets still upstairs in room 303. The vision of the girl cut to pieces flashing like pop-ups in his mind. A crime scene tape across the door. Two uniform cops standing outside the door. The walls grimy. The nylon carpet, thin, sticky, and stained

A sea of people moves back and forth under the neon haze. Strip club spruikers shouting, people laughing, threatening, drunk, stoned, wide-eyed, and sober. Tourists, mums and dads, wild suburban boys and girls all out for the party. It is insane what has happened.

He wears black jeans; a black long-sleeved shirt; hard, thick black shoes on his feet. He is handsome with strong cheekbones, solidly built with light brown hair. The smoking hasn't damaged him yet.

He hears the switchboard ringing, quickly shuts and locks the front door. He reaches over the reception desk, the cigarette pressed firmly between two fingers in his left hand, hits answer with the middle finger of his right hand, picks up the handset.

'Cross Motel.'

'What happened?'

It's the owner, Mick.

'You have to come in.'

'Bullshit I do. What happened?'

'A junkie, a working girl, her trick cut her to pieces. It was fuck...'

'Paying guest?'

The night manager swallows, takes a quick hit of his cigarette, smoke blowing out his nose and mouth when he says, 'You know my deal with Katya.'

'But it wasn't Katya, was it? It was some junkie whore friend of Katya you let use the room for free. Or you charged her, pocketed the money, and now the cops are there. The media might turn up too if it's a quiet night.'

'Cops don't care about freebie motel rooms.'

'You know that the law *does* care. That's right *the law* says that everyone's got to register, and did you know that *by law*, I'm supposed to keep those registration cards for seven years.'

'Sorry, Mick.'

'You getting any PI work?'

'Not a lot.'

'You might need some and a good lawyer. You're on your own on this one,' he says and hangs up.

Someone is knocking on the front door.

The night manager turns and looks. It's two suits with cop written all over them and three other guys. Behind them, two guests from Albury, who were earlier asking him about the Mardi Gras even though it was winter and the Mardi Gras was in March.

He unlocks the door. He can't quit this job. Would Mick sack him? He needs the money to stay afloat. The Albury tourists gawk. The three guys line up at the lift in front of the tourists.

'Who are they?' The night manager asks the bigger suit.

'Forensic boys.'

'Where are their suits and little shoes and...'

'They'll put them on upstairs,' the bigger detective says, 'that alright with you, boss?'

Travis says nothing.

The guests get in the lift with them. The two detectives look at Travis, the bigger guy again says, 'Got your guest list up to date?'

'I'll print one for you.'

Both cops carry guns — the bigger guy carries his on his hip, the other guy has a shoulder holster. Travis goes back to the front door, locks it. Comes around behind the reception desk and the bigger guy with red hair says, 'I'm DI Olsen, this is DC Lynch,' he says pointing to his offsider.

Olsen has pale, almost translucent, white skin to match his red hair. His bicep muscles press hard against the black suit. He has a thick, bull-like neck from working out; a gym junkie or ex-rugby league player. Dangerous looking man. He stands round-shouldered, says, 'What's your name?'

'Travis Whyte.'

'Travis? Haven't heard of a Travis before.'

'Haven't heard that before.'

'Got balls too, Travis.'

Travis doesn't say anything. Olsen shrugs his big shoulders, stares blankly at Travis, says, 'What the fuck happened, Travis?'

'The girl took a trick up to her room. About ten minutes later I hear screaming, but I don't know if it's inside or outside,' he says flinging his arm out in the direction of the street, 'then again, the screaming; loud, wild screaming. I go for the stairs, bolt up to 303. Must be the hooker. The door is wide open. I see her lying on the bed, cuts and blood all over her. She's frozen still, bleeding so much... The sheets already soaked in blood. I'm hyperventilating, standing by the bed, no sign of the guy. I turn around. He's in the doorway, the trick, with a knife. He points it at me. He's wearing black gloves, runs the knife slowly across his throat, no expression, but turns and runs. I ring the ambos.'

'You said he had no blood on him?'

'Yeah, I don't get that. He had a backpack he held by his left shoulder.'

'No blood on him?'

'No.'

'You try and help the girl?'

'I talked to her, talked crap about football, cricket, anything. I held her hand, told her that she was going to make it, told her to hang on. Kept talking until the ambos arrived.'

'What about you? You don't have any blood on you either?'

'I changed. I had these clothes with me for going out later.'

'Where are the clothes you had on when you were in the room.'

'In a plastic bag in the back office,' he says pointing behind him.

'What happened when you checked her in?' Olsen asks.

'It was a cash job. We agreed on $120 for the room. The guy paid.'

'He get a good look at you.'

'Yes.'

'You got a registration card?'

'No.'

Cops look at each other, say nothing.

The switchboard starts ringing. A guest is knocking on the door. The night manager answers the phone. Lynch opens the door, vets the guests with the guest list, then lets them up in the lift. The night manager puts the handset down, enquiry fixed. Olsen repeats his question.

'You get a good look at him?'

'Yeah, he was right in front of me.'

'He knows you work here, now...'

'I know what you're getting at. We don't have CCTV, but the council must on Darlinghurst Road, you can get...'

'You telling me my job, again, boss?'

'No.'

'What time do you knock off?'

'Half-an-hour from now. 11pm.'

'Give me the plastic bag with your clothes. The lab boys will test them. I'll walk you down to the station after you knock off, for a statement, and we'll get you to do an identikit of the attacker.'

Travis nods but thinks, fuck this. I don't need this shit. The guy saw me. He fucken saw me. He's out there somewhere.

'John, we go upstairs now,' Olsen says to Lynch.

Silence inside the small reception area, but always the constant buzz of people outside the door, yelling, laughing; craziness.

The street on fire.

The switchboard rings again. He hits the answer button hard, says, 'Cross Motel.'

'Travis.'

'Ahn, is that you?'

'Yes, you have to help me find Billy.'

'Oh wow, Ahn, tonight of all nights, you ring me. Oh shit. You want me to find Billy? What the fuck is that?'

'He's missing. It's what you do. You find people. I'll pay your daily rate.'

'You mean your father will.'

'Whatever, I need you.'

'How long has he been missing?'

'Ten days.'

'Oh fuck, Billy might be doing what Billy does.'

Travis thinks, even for Billy, this is too long to not even contact Ahn. Then he thinks of the money. Who is running Billy's club? He might be able to string the search out for a while.

'Travis?'

'I'm not feeling that great, Ahn. Big trouble in the motel tonight. Cops. All kinds of shit.'

'What happened?'

'I'll tell you later.'

'Come over when you knock off. I'll give you the key to Billy's place. He doesn't disappear like that anymore, he's changed. You might find something at his place to...'

'I get it. I'll pick up the keys after I speak to the cops. But only for you. If it was anybody else.'

'Thanks, Travis.'

'I'll call you when I'm done with the cops.'

———

Olsen walks him to the Kings Cross Police Station, buys him coffee on the way. The night manager does an identikit.

'He was uh, medium height, short brown hair, his face, it, I don't know, he was nothing special. Plain. He was plain and boring. Black or blue jeans. I can get him in my mind now, a brown jumper with a check shirt. I could see the collar, nothing else.'

'Was he big? A thickset kind of guy,' Olsen asks him.

'No, he was normal, not overweight, not big, not fat. I hate to say it, but he was, nothing stood out.

On and on he goes.

Olsen takes Travis from the small room, his hand in the small of his back, guides him into a smaller office. Lynch joins them. Olsen takes his gun off his hip, puts it on the desk, stares straight into Travis's soul, says slowly, firmly, 'I want to know, Travis. Why no registration card? Why was this transaction cash? No receipts, no paperwork at all.'

'I do it sometimes.'

'Do what?'

'Cash transactions an...'

'I spoke to your boss, Mick, he said you have an arrangement with a street girl, Katya. This right?'

'Yes.'

'Where is she?'

'Don't know.'

'I don't believe you, Travis.'

'That's your business.'

In his mind, Travis could see Katya in her spot across the road from the Cross Motel front door. Where was she?

'You checked a guest in. A prostitute. There was a used needle in the room. No registration card. No record of them, and ten minutes later she's cut to pieces in room 303. Her name is Ann, Travis, she has a mother out there somewhere.'

'No comment.'

'You are in deep shit, Travis.'

'No comment.'

CHAPTER TWO

Travis walks out of the police station. Olsen had hit him with question after question. Like a front-row forward in a state-of-origin game, buttering up again and again. Travis took the hits with a no comment, then Lynch started in with the accusations.

'You're a thief. Cheating on your boss. A rat, stealing money from him. A girl is lying near dead. You need to say something.'

'No comment.'

He needed a lawyer. Ahn could find him one. Pay for it too.

The truth is he is flat broke and needed the $120 to keep him going until payday. His list of bad habits almost always has him teetering on the brink of going under.

At the top of the stairs leading to the concrete of Fitzroy Gardens, his finds it a little hard to breathe. He stops and bends down. He can't breathe, he struggles trying to catch some air. Sits down on his arse gasping for air. Embarrassed as fuck. Can't catch a breath, he puts his hand across his chest, tries to suck in air, at last, a breath, a few more deep breaths. He kneels, stands. Holds his arm across his chest, breathes in deeply, then breathes out slowly, counting, one and two and three and four and five. Repeats it in the middle of the park twice more. His breathing back to normal. He sighs. Something he learnt from the New York Times online.

He walks slowly back to the Cross. Gavin, the night porter, does a sideline dealing in speed, and Travis needs some. Gavin will give him credit. He has to find three people. Katya had been with Perry when she rang. Asking for a free room for Ann. Travis saw dollar signs. Straight away he knew he would pocket the cash for the room for gambling and drinking money. Perry is bad news, a male cross-dresser. Travis doesn't properly know; doesn't care. Perry is also a smack and speed dealer and worst of all, a pimp. Trading in misery. Katya adores Perry who in turn feeds her smack habit with free gear. Can they have known the attacker all along? Find Katya. Find Perry. Find the attacker. Because he doesn't want the guy finding him. Maybe he was watching now. That knife concealed.

Travis hustles back across the square, past the El Alamein fountain, eyes darting left and right back up into the mess of The Cross. People buzzing, shooting all around him, in his space. It is freezing. He has his laptop, the laptop bag-strap across his chest, making him look like an office worker or geek or worse. Travis is from Melbourne. He is twenty-two. When he was nineteen, he was on the radar of all the AFL clubs, he was going to be drafted, a first-round pick for sure, top five, until the night before the draft when his world came tumbling down. He escaped to Sydney, got his Private Enquiry Agent license after doing a course in a function room above a motel in Kingsford. Told himself he was working in the crappy motel only until he could afford to be a PI full time. He *could* find people. He had a sort of rep for it. Only the jobs were spaced too far apart.

He snorts two lines in the back office of the Cross Motel. Takes two one-gram bags with him. Time to find these people. His car is parked in a car park on Ward Ave in an apartment building. The owner lets staff of the motel park there. He is a friend of Mick's. He opens the door of his white Triumph Dolomite Sprint. This model of Triumph is fast. The previous owner had told him there was something extra too, under the hood, Travis knew nothing about engines, but he test drove it and it flew. It was old and clunky but fast; the Millennium Falcon on the streets of Sydney. He shot out of the driveway onto Ward Ave and drove fast as he could to Bondi.

Ahn opened the door wide, wearing a black dress, red lipstick, and nothing else.

'You going to let me in?'

She stands to one side. He slowly brushes past her into the hallway. She closes the door and turns and put her arms round his neck, nuzzles her face against his shoulder then kisses him on the neck. He smiles and says, 'Nice welcome,' and leans down and kisses her on her red lips, and she kisses him back hard, passionately. He lifts her up, pushes her against the wall and she reaches for his shirt, undoing the buttons, pulling it out of his pants, ripping at the belt. It comes apart. She tears the button on his trousers off. The laptop bag-strap breaks and it thumps to the floor. She grabs his hard cock, whispers in his ear, 'Fuck me now'. He feels her wetness under the dress and pushes inside her, her arse flat against the wall, his hands pinning hers to the wall. They fuck hard, and he almost slips, half laughs but keeps stroking in and out. Ahn pushing back against him, he thrusts harder, faster, dripping with sweat now, burning up. Ahn growling, he keeps thrusting harder, faster, she pumps back, and he comes inside her but stays hard, thrusting again and again so she can come. He lets her hands go and she grabs his hair, his face, groaning out loud, he grabs her small bum and scratches his fingernails into her skin, and she comes hard, and they both collapse in a heap in the hallway, and she says, 'Oh, fuck that was good.'

Travis says nothing, gets his breath back. Stares straight ahead, the speed, running hard in his brain, all through his veins, almost electrified, but he knows what he has to do.

'Ahn, give me the keys to Billy's place. I need a week upfront into my bank account. I'll text you the details. I need a lawyer by tomorrow. I'm sorry, I need to go. Need to find Katya.'

'The prostitute. Why? What did she do?'

'Best you don't know anything. Three hundred a day. Tomorrow or tonight. First seven days in advance.'

He stands up, pulls his briefs up, still semi-hard, pulls up his pants, tucks himself in.

'Ahn, keys to Billy's place. I got to go.'

'I haven't seen you this scared, this worried, not since Melbourne.'

'Keys, Ahn, for fuck's sake.'

'Alright.' She stands up and walks quickly to her bedroom to get the keys.

CHAPTER THREE

Travis sits in his car. In the car park on Ward Ave. He tries Katya's mobile. Voicemail. He gets out and walks down the stairs and exits to Ward Ave, walks quickly along to Bayswater Road and turns right. Katya sometimes hangs out in the Kardomah Café. They have free entry on Thursday night. Decent bands. He walks down the stairs into the subterranean band room. A band plays some perfect pop music. Travis searches the room with his eyes. Can't see her. Walks to the bar. Gets a double vodka with lots of ice, sips it, walks through the mostly under-thirty crowd, searching, but she isn't here. He goes right down the back of the room, stands on a table, and his eyes dart all over the place. No, not here. One last thing. He knocks on the door of the female toilets and walks in, two girls doing their make-up don't even look up. All four cubicle doors are closed. He knocks on each door calling her name out, 'Katya, Katya'. Nothing.

He leaves quickly and walks to Darlinghurst Road. Crosses over the street towards the Crest Hotel bottle shop. About fifty metres past it is a set of stairs. He walks down. It is an old video games parlour, but all that remains now is a glass office and bare space. A door in the far corner leading to what he didn't know. Some young people are huddled together in the far corner in the semi-dark. Empty fits scattered all over the floor. In the glass office, a sixteen-year-old Aboriginal boy sits on an orange swivel chair. Travis walks over to him. He knows the boy from around The Cross. They talked AFL before. Travis had told him he was on the radar to be drafted; it was something he never told anyone, but the kid was AFL crazy. Travis still plays, only it is for Randwick, a million miles from the big league.

The boy says, 'What'd you want?'

'I'm looking for Katya.'

'Bad shit at the Cross I hear,' the boy says.

'Katya, she here or not?'

The boy points at the door in the far corner of the room.

Travis walks to it, tries to pull it open, it doesn't budge an inch. The young boy laughs, and the other people in the room laugh, and Travis wheels around and runs at the boy, the speed pushing him hard. He tries to open the door to the office, but it doesn't move an inch, and they all laugh again. Travis picks up a lone chair and swings it hard, and the glass shatters, and the boy falls off his swivel chair but gets up calmly and says, 'Go. Katya's not here, go.'

Travis emerges back on Darlinghurst Road. There is another place she might be, further along, before you reach Springfield Park, next door to a motel almost as shitty as the Cross. He climbs the stairs up to the peep show. Katya works here sometimes when she is desperate. They have a set up like in Paris Texas. You put money in a slot, and a panel opens, and a girl performs in front of you like Natassja Kinski did with Harry Dean-Stanton. It is weirdly brilliant, but the place is filthy, and there are video booths set up where you can do the same thing. Slot dollar coins and watch hardcore porno. Toilet paper on a hook to clean yourself up after finishing.

Travis goes to the counter where a bored clerk asks him how many coins he wants. Travis says, 'I'm looking for Katya.'

His mobile rings as the guy says, 'Don't know any girls names, I just work...'

'Yeah, you just work here,' and Travis answers his mobile. It is the cop, Olsen.

'Ann is dead, Travis. The girl couldn't survive the knife attack. This is murder now. I need to speak to you again.'

'Alright. I'll come in tomorrow.'

'Need you to do that as soon as you've had some sleep. Sooner. This is murder, Travis.'

'You said that. Be there at 1 or 2 pm after some sleep.'

'Make sure of it.'

Olsen hangs up. Travis didn't kill her. The cop knows that but he... he thinks Travis knows more.

Travis walks to the booth where the girls dance live, feeds some coins in. The panel opens, but it isn't Katya.

He sticks his hand under the panel, to hold it open, says, 'Katya, I need to see her, It's urgent.'

Travis is shocked when the girl says,

'She's in the private room, down the hallway.'

He turns around, opens the door, looks around, finds the hallway, walks along. There is an open door. A girl sits slumped in an old torn armchair, nodding on and off, high on heroin, needle marks in the crook of both arms. For a split second, he thinks it is Katya, but it isn't. She is too far gone this one. Katya is a junkie, but a functioning one.

'Where's Katya?' He says loudly.

'I'm Katya,' the girl says, smiling sickly at him. 'I'm Mary Lou and the skipper too on Gilligan's Island.'

Travis shakes his head, 'Fuck this.'

He turns and walks out onto the stairs.

The Aboriginal boy from the shooting gallery is sitting on the top step.

'Hey, Mr Footballer.'

'Hey, sorry about the chair.'

'Not my place, only hang out there. Perry knows the knifeman.'

'What?'

'Katya's friend, the pimp, dealer, he knows.'

'How do you know this?'

'He talks to me afterwards when he's relaxed, know what I mean?'

'He pays you.'

'Yeah.'

'For sex?'

'Whatever you want to call it.'

'What did...'

'He told me there was a guy wanted to do that shit. It was a few days ago. I don't know anything else, but like I said, Perry knows someone that wanted this. Must.'

'What's your name, kid?'

'Whatever you want it to be. I won't say nothing to the cops. Tell them I never met you, footballer.'

'Ok, alright.'

His mobile rings again.

'Hello,' a distant voice says.

'Katya, where the fuck are...'

'You tell the cops it was me that sent Ann.'

'Where are you?'

'Hey! You tell the cops that...'

'I told them I don't where you are, but they know. Mick told them I gave you a free room'

'Shit.'

'Katya, she's dead. Ann is dead.'

'I need a place to stay.'

Travis felt in his pocket for the keys to Billy's place. Pressed his fingers through his pants onto them.

'I got a place for you. Where's Perry?'

'Don't know. Where's this place?'

He gave her Billy's address in Darlinghurst, saying, 'I'll be there in ten minutes.'

'Thanks, Travis, I owe you.'

Travis looks at the young boy and says, 'I play at Randwick, you want to come down for a game, let me know. You know where I work. Might change your life.'

'Like it changed yours,' the boy says.

Travis shrugs and starts walking down the stairs. When he gets to the bottom step the boy yells out, 'Might do it. Might come for a game.'

CHAPTER FOUR

Billy lives on Surrey Street, two blocks back from the bustling café strip of Victoria Street. Travis parks his car out the front. Opens the front door to Billy's place. He is close. Katya will be here soon. She will lead him to Perry. He shakes his head, and a foul smell hits him as he walks down the hallway to the kitchen. There is water seeping out from under the fridge. He tries to turn on the lights. The power is off. He walks back down the hallway to the fuse box. Everything is switched on. What the hell? He hears it start to rain heavily and shivers. His mobile rings.

'Yes.'

'I'm outside.'

'Right.'

He opens the door, and Katya is there. Damp, short blond hair, wet round face, nose from a Picasso painting, her beauty preserved rather than destroyed by the drugs. But for how long? He pulls her in out of the rain. It is thumping down.

'It only started raining a few seconds ago, and I'm soaked.'

'Come. Come. There should be clothes in the bedroom.'

He takes her hand and leads her down the hallway. She is

wearing a short denim skirt, black leggings. A black camisole over a purple bra. Her hair is multi-coloured with a fringe above her blue eyes. Travis has stared into them often, laughing with her many times as she told him stories about all the mad stuff she got up to.

He might be in love with her.

She finds a blue flannelette shirt and a pair of track pants in the closet, strips off unashamedly. Travis looking, turning away, and then looking back as she puts them on.

'The power has been cut off.'

'Whose place is this?'

'Billy, a friend of Ahn. I told you about Ahn. He's missing. We have to talk now. I need to know where Perry is.'

'Shit. Fuck. I'm sorry about Ann, I didn't know... how could I know?'

Tears run down her cheeks.

Travis wonders whether she might be the consummate actor. She lives her whole life conning people. But this kind of evil?

'Perry. Where is he, she? Whatever the fuck.'

'I don't know,' she says, sniffling now, more tears, 'he moves from one place to another every few days. I went back to the Hotel where he was in Surry Hills, but he'd checked out. That's when I rang you.'

'Where does she... oh fuck. What is she? He? What do I call her?'

'He. He only dresses as a female.'

'You sound...'

She starts crying again, says, 'Ann was a baby. Only a kid.'

'Why'd you want the free room, Katya? I need to know.'

'You can't possibly think... I. No, you don't think that. Don't you dare.'

'Not you, Perry. Again. How can I find him?'

'I fucken told you. He moves all over the place. More than ever now with Airbnb. He's either broke or loaded. No in-between.'

'Did he ask you to get the room for free? Did he know the guy with Ann?'

'Don't ask me again, Travis. I can feel the accusation in your voice. Please stop it. You're scaring me.'

'OK, OK. I have some weed. Want to get stoned?'

'Oh yes, please.'

Travis rolls the joint. He'll have to go through the whole place looking for clues to see where Billy is. Not tonight though. He's done. A big smoke with Katya, then sleep.'

CHAPTER FIVE

Travis wakes with a jolt. His eyes pop open. Where the fuck am I, he thinks? He looks around, his mind not locked into gear, looking for something that identifies where he is. Then it hits him like a freight train. He feels short of breath. The image of the girl cut to pieces. His heart starts racing, he takes deep breaths. Remembers his technique. Places his hand over his chest, deep breath in, deep breath out slowly, counting it down from five to one and again and again. He can breathe normally now but reaches for his cigarettes on the chest-of-drawers next to the bed. Can't find a lighter.

Gets out of bed, grabs his jeans off the floor, picks up his black shirt. The lighter drops to the floor. He does the buttons on the shirt up, tucks himself in. Bloody Ahn ripped off his button. He lights his cigarette, blows the smoke straight out. He'll have to do a coffee and croissant run to Victoria Street. He inhales smoke from his Stuyvesant cigarette, blows it straight out, smiling. He loves smoking, feels like he can get away with it, playing in the low grade for Randwick, a million miles from what could have been. He only started smoking when he moved to Sydney when he knew no-one would take a chance on him again.

He knocks on the door to Billy's room. No answer. Knocks again and walks in, but Katya is gone. Fuck her. How is he going to find Perry? He walks down the hall. The front door is open. Sweet fucken Jesus. If that killer was around, watching? It hits him. Would he have taken Katya? Could he? Did he sleep that heavily? He rings Katya. Amazingly she answers,

'Hey, partner, thanks for last night. Listen, sorry I...'

'You left the bloody front door open.'

'Oh, did I. Um, I needed my fix baby. Got the cramps last night about 3 am. Had to bolt.'

'Perry?'

'I told you, Travis. If I find him. And I will see him, sometime, I always do. I'll ring you straight away.'

She ended the call.

Travis called Ahn.

'Travis, where are you?'

'Billy's place. The power is off. Can you get it turned back on?'

'If I know Billy he forgot to pay the bill. I think he's with Simply Energy. I'll call them.'

'I haven't got time to do anything until tonight. I'll come back here after training. Go through the whole place, look for something that might tell us where he is.'

'What about now?'

'I have to go back to see the cops. The girl died. It's murder. I need a lawyer. I know you can find me...'

'Angelo Puglisi.'

'That came out quick.'

'He's brilliant. Jason Weaver mentored him. Now he works for Andy Chui. Don't you know him?'

'No.'

'My father knows them both. He's a great guy and a man on the rise. He did the Simon Law case.'

'The drug dealer?'

'Alleged.'

'Got him off.'

'Yes. What time do you have to see the police?'

'Early afternoon. Listen, meet me at Gabby's in half-an-hour for breakfast.'

'I have to go to work.'

'Blow them off.'

'I work for...'

'I know who you work for. Take a couple of hours off. Menstrual fucking leave or something.'

'Or something,' Ahn says and starts laughing. 'Menstrual bloody...'

'Ha Ha, sorry. I'm not kosher with that... Shit. Only be there, huh?'

Travis ends the call. It is 9 am.

He left the apartment as it was, still stinking from the rotted food in the fridge. He'd do it all when he came back. When the power was back on. He closed the front door, looked around. A guy walking one of those beautiful brown labs. Some schoolgirls walking and talking a million miles an hour, totally oblivious to him, even as he walks in front of them and gets in the Triumph. He turns the key in the ignition, and his mobile rings. He looks down at the passenger seat where the phone sits, sees Mick's name on the screen. He turns the car off and answers,

'Mick.'

'Yeah, Travis, spoke to the cops last night and this morning. The poor girl is dead.'

'Yep.'

'That's it, yep?'

Travis says nothing. A few seconds tick over, but it feels like two or three minutes to Travis, and still, he keeps his mouth shut.

Mick says, 'Gotta let you go, mate. The whole cash in hand, no rego card business, put me right in the shit, mate.'

'Understand, Mick. Appreciate the opportunity you...'

'C'mon Travis, it's a nothing job, you can do better.'

'I'm not too proud, Mick. I needed the cash, still do.
'Right. Stay in touch, mate.'
The call ends.
Mick calling him mate, mate, fucken mate.

He starts the car again, drives fast to Victoria Street, turns left, guns the car down to Oxford Street, past the hospital where Ann died. On Oxford Street, he rips through the gears first to fourth accelerating super quick, then cruising in fifth. He pops the Hoodoo Gurus into the deck, turns the volume up high all the way to Campbell Parade, finds a park outside the surf shop, about one-hundred metres from Gabby's café.

He walks into the café. Ahn is already there. She stands up. She has shaved her head to a number two razor cut from the night before. Wears red cords, an orange t-shirt with the cotton clinging to the outline of her small, round breasts, her nipples also pressing the cotton. Travis says,

'You still don't fuck around, do you?'
'You know me.'
'Yeah, I know *you*.'
'But, I like it. I feel empowered.'
'That's the burn the bra thing you've nailed. You look like a dyke. A sexy dyke.'
'Thanks, I think.'
'How'd you go with work?'
'I took the day off. You won't believe this, but I've been there for eighteen months, and this is my first sickie.'
'Do you remember the first time we came here. When we first hit town, what, two-and-half-years-ago.'
'I remember. Look, about last night I...'
'I get it, Ahn. Frustration.'
'Bloody Billy. I went through his house, but nothing looked weird.'

Travis thinks she probably walked from room to room without even opening a drawer.

'Right, I'll get onto it. I have to go home, change clothes after we're done here. I might have time to look around before seeing the cops. What about this guy Puglisi?'

'He'll meet you in the Fountain Café at 12.30.'

'Oh, right. Good. What's he look like?'

'Tall, slim, expensive suit, ponytail.'

'Rocking the ponytail in court, interesting.'

The waitress, a tall willowy blond creature, stands next to their table. They order the breaky special with a strong flat white for Travis and green tea for Ahn.

'Did you argue with Billy?'

'Nothing. Nothing big anyhow. I don't get it. I don't. I...'

'I can see you're worried, not calm, which is not you.'

'Please, find him.'

'I will, don't worry. I'll text you my bank account and BSB. I need the cash.'

'I have your details from when I lent you that money last summer...'

'Oh yeah, good thing I paid you back.'

'I've been trying not to say anything, but what're doing Travis? Still in that seedy little job and now with that girl murdered last night. Did you see her? Are you involved?'

'I gotta give you a no comment on all of that. I know you probably saw it on the news, but I can't say anything.'

'Like that, huh?'

'For your information, I got sacked sitting in my car outside Billy's place earlier, so don't worry about me slumming as Night Manager in The Cross anymore.'

Ahn puts her hand on his forearm, he looks into her coal-black eyes, sees she is genuinely upset. They finish eating and drinking, Travis says, 'What're going to do on your first sickie?'

'Might go to Newtown. Do some clothes shopping. Catch up with Tara after that.'

'She's not working?'

'No. Tara doesn't work.'

Ahn lives in North Bondi, Travis offers her a lift, but she says, 'Nah, I'll walk. Let me know how it pans out?'

'Will do.'

They kiss goodbye in the entrance to the café. Travis walks to his car, jumps in, turns his phone back on. A message from Olsen. Be at Kings Cross Police Station at 1 pm for a formal interview. Travis sighs. Drives the short distance to his apartment on Lamrock Ave, walks up the steep stairs, down the side path to his front door, unlocks it, pushes the door open. Stuffy but neat and tidy. He'd had a weekly clean up before work yesterday. It seemed more than a day ago, more like a week ago. Shit, he forgot to ask Ahn about the power. He made a quick call, and she told him it was back on. The bill had been unpaid for three months, and Billy got a monthly bill. What the fuck was that son-of-a-bitch up to?

He checks his bank account balance through his phone app. Ahn has already put the $2,100 in. He smiles. Fuck Billy's place. He'll do that after training. He isn't working anymore. It is 10.30 am. He has a shower, dresses in Black Levi's, black T-shirt, blue hoodie, slips into some royal blue Nike's, runs down to the car, and drives fast, as always, to The Cross, parks in the apartment building on Ward Ave. They haven't changed the code on him, yet.

He walks quickly to the ATM next to the Crest Hotel on Darlinghurst Road and withdraws five hundred, walks fast, like he's late for a job interview, down the Crest Hotel Arcade, into the TAB at the top of Victoria Street. He has an hour or more to play on the horses and greyhounds before meeting Angelo Puglisi. He fills out the first betting slip of the day, and as he is about to turn and walk to the counter his heart starts beating fast, he can't breathe. The knifeman comes into his mind, the killer, whatever you want to call him. Travis has been busy. Forgotten about the man. He sits down, puts his hand over his chest, does his breathing exercises, slowly returns to normal. The guy behind the glass screens says, 'Are you alright, mate? You looked in a bit of trouble there."

Travis sticks the form in the machine, takes his ticket from the old bloke and says, 'I'm alright, thanks for asking.'

He stands outside, smoking, watching the race run, looking around now, he was in the killer's territory, but it was Travis' territory too. He's been working there for two-and-half years, ever since he arrived in Sydney, and at night, right in the heart of The Cross. Come find me you gutless prick, he thinks. His mobile rings. His dad. He flicks it to voicemail.

His horse runs second, but he had one hundred on the nose. Travis doesn't believe in place or each-way bets. He searches the form guides in New Zealand, the local races at Taree, further north to Brisbane, looking for the big outsider. Thinking about Ann. Her body cut to shreds. The killer looking him in the eye. If he is watching him, he would have struck at Billy's place with the door open wide. Fucken Katya and that prick Perry. Where was he? But then, Travis thought, he would have lost the guy when he drove to Ahn's place *if* he had been following him.

CHAPTER SIX

Travis walks into the Fountain Café, looks around, can't see the guy, sits at the window on Darlinghurst Road, happy to have no-one around or behind him. His mobile rings again. His dad again. He flicks it again. Angelo Puglisi walks along the street past him into the café. He looks around, Travis waves at him.

Angelo with long black hair tied in a man bun, expensive black suit, sky blue shirt, black silk tie, he stands straight-backed, sticks out his hand as he reaches the table. Travis stands up, shakes his hand, Angelo says, 'Travis, rough twenty-four hours for you.'

'Yeah, not even twenty-four, more shit's going to happen now.'

They sit.

'What can you tell me?'

Travis goes through the story, including the phone call he got from Katya, his suspicions about Perry, the Aboriginal boy, what he also said about Perry. Tracking back to the kill. Finding Ann cut up, the killer eyeballing him, imitating slashing the knife across his throat. His talk with Katya at Billy's place. He told him about his current job looking for Billy. Angelo smiles at this. Travis tells him he doesn't want Katya brought into this. He thinks Perry is the key to finding the guy.

'Travis, Ahn told me you're a private investigator.

'Yeah, I am.'

'I appreciate you want to find the guy who killed Ann because you're scared, but my advice is to be cautious. Don't say anything to the police that you haven't already. I'm glad you told me everything, though, Your concerns about Katya.'

'What now?'

'We go in there. They start to grill us. I say to them that my client is not obliged to answer any questions, and that's how it goes. They ask you a question, you don't say anything, I say, my client is not obliged to answer any questions. We cool?' he says smiling.

'Yeah, we're cool.'

'Let's go, then.'

They sit opposite Olsen and Lynch, and they read him his rights, begin the interview. Olsen starts.

'Travis, Ann Gables is dead. You checked her into the Cross Motel last night without a registration card. Why?'

'My client is not obliged to answer any questions.'

That's the way it went for twenty minutes. Travis felt himself getting hotter and hotter. He did want to help, he thought he could help, but he took his lawyer's advice, then it took a different tack.

'You were going to be the superstar, weren't you Travis?'

Angelo looks at Travis who shrugs and looks down.

'But it all went south, didn't it? Golden boy. Going to be top five, maybe top three, maybe the number one draft pick. Travis Whyte of the Oakleigh Chargers. But you fucked up Travis, like you fucken fucked up last night, you little piece of fucken shit. I want answers. That girl is dead. Start fucken talking, you little prick.'

Angelo looks at Travis but says slowly to Olsen,

'My client is not obliged to answer any questions.'

'My arse he's not obliged. Get the fuck out of here, both of you. I'm not done with you, Travis, not by a fucken long shot, hero.'

Travis and Angelo walk out of the Kings Cross police station. Travis takes out his cigarettes, grabs one out of the pack, pulls the lighter from his pocket, puts flame to the cigarette, draws the smoke in deeply, exhales the smoke into the cool, crisp air.

The sky is dirty-washing grey, they stand together for a few minutes, then Angelo says, 'That true about you being a top five in the draft?'

'Yep.'

'What happened? What was Olsen on about?'

'Maybe another time, I'll tell you.'

'You were pretty cool in there, Travis. A lot of guys would have wanted to blurt out their story and...'

'I can take instructions. I did my PEA course. I know the number one rule is to say nothing. I pretty much said nothing last night.'

'Good training.'

'Yeah, it's funny, Ahn has got me chasing Billy. He's missing. You know, Billy?'

'Only by reputation. I think my employer, Mr Chui, I think he might like you.

'Mr Chui I know by reputation.'

'Yes. You already know this area. You've been working at night here for two or three years.'

'If you've got work, please ring me. I can't thank you enough for today. I have to go, got footy training.'

'You still play?'

'Love the game.'

Angelo puts his hand out again. Travis shakes it, saying, 'Gotta go, man. Nice to meet you,' and he rushes up the stairs, across the concrete park, past the Fountain Café, his eyes, darting left and right. He stops outside the Cross Motel. Sees Mick sitting at the reception desk. He wouldn't like that. Always thought it was beneath him to work on the desk. Travis kept walking fast, left down Roslyn Street to Ward Ave, to his car. He would train hard, bust his gut running and tackling, try and get his kicking and handballing as precise as he could.

CHAPTER SEVEN

Travis ran and bounced the football at the same time, making it bounce straight back into his chest, expertly. It starts to lightly rain, the wind picking up. He looks around, hoping the Aboriginal kid turned up, but he was nowhere to be seen. He might look him up again tonight. Perry and Katya still doing his head in.

Some of the guys ask him about the attack at the Cross. He tells them he can't say anything. The club president comes into the rooms after training, has a word with his star player, asks if he'll be alright for the game on Sunday. Travis smiles and laughs, says, 'Sure, boss, good as gold.'

After training, he drives to his place in Bondi, picks up a weeks' worth of change of clothes, some CDs and DVDs. A small bag of weed from the drawer in his kitchen. Drives through the bottle shop at the Bondi Hotel, picks up a bottle of Vodka. At Billy's the power is back on. He puts on Lou Reed loud, hits the kitchen, cleans it like a pro. Throws all the rotting food, empty milk, and other drink containers in the bin out in the small square space of the back courtyard, wheels them out the front, out of smelling distance.

Then he has a shower, puts on black Levi's, a black t-shirt with

Studio Weekend written across the chest in white. Black Docs, a red Levi's trucker jacket. Checks himself in the mirror. The thick cheekbones, his light brown hair is getting longer. He thinks of Ahn shaving her head overnight on a whim. No hairdresser necessary. Rolls a joint. Takes the Vodka out of the fridge, pours a large measure into a shot glass, sips it, lights the joint, and smoke drifts up and all around him, and he finishes the Vodka shot, takes deep drags on the joint until it becomes a roach, stabs it out into a copper ashtray. Stands up, turns around and walks out into the hallway, down to Billy's room.

He opens the top drawer of the chest-of-drawers beside the bed. Underwear and socks. He rifles through the underwear, finds nothing. Does the same with the rolled-up socks, finds two small coin bags, white powder in them. He wets his middle finger with his tongue, dips it into one of the baggies. It is speed, not coke, so maybe he wasn't doing as well as Ahn thought, although he knew people who liked speed better. If it was ice, you'd be worried. The second drawer was white t-shirts, maybe ten. Travis dug his hands in and at the bottom of the pile was a diary, also a handwritten letter addressed to *Dear Billy*. He folds the letter to put in the diary to read later then stops himself. Goes to the bottom of the letter, it is signed, *love Jeffy*. Travis reads the whole thing; it is a love letter. Billy swinging both ways nowadays. The diary could wait until he had searched everywhere else.

There was nothing else in the second or third drawers. He went to the built-in closet, starting pulling the hangers back, slowly, one by one. A couple of black sports jackets. He looks at the label. Uniqlo, the Japanese clothing store. Not expensive but look expensive. He put his hands in all the pockets, came out with a foil of what looked like a Thai Buddha stick. You didn't get this stuff anymore. It is weed, all thick sticky heads, with thread tying it to a thin stick of wood. Travis smells it. It is pungent. He thinks to himself again, you don't get this stuff anymore. My old man used to tell me about it.

He found cash in pants and other jackets, about three hundred all up. A careless man or simply doing well, maybe? His mobile rings, a number he doesn't know, he answers.

'Hello.'

'Travis, Angelo Puglisi.'

'Yep.'

'Can you meet with Mr Chui on Sunday for lunch?'

'I'm playing footy.'

'Alright, I'll get back to you. You alright?'

'Yeah.'

'Did you find your friend Katya? Or the other one, Perry?'

'No, but you've reminded me to keep calling Katya. I need a few minutes with Perry. I think I...'

'Remember what I said; let the police do their job. If you find this person, this Perry, ring me and I'll call Olsen, tell him where Perry is, and you stay clear of it all.'

'Right, you're right. I will. I can meet Mr Chui tomorrow but not Sunday.'

'I'll call you back.'

Travis presses end on his mobile. Rings Katya straight away. Voicemail. Shit.

His mobile rings again. His dad. Shit. He was a prick for not calling him.

'Hi, dad.'

'Travis, I saw what happened on the news. Are you clear of it? No trouble?'

'No dad, no trouble. You know the media; they blow it up.'

'Yes. You hear from your mother?'

'No, I'll ring her.'

'You playing on the week...'

'Yeah, big game against Maroubra. Second v third.'

'Remember your goals. Thirty disposals a game and...'

'I got it; you say the same thing every fortnight.'

'Do you get your thirty dis...'

'Yeah, yeah. What about you?'

'I'm running every two or three days, started doing some bush walks, two hours out, two hours back. Marysville, Dandenong Ranges, and Sherbrooke. It's beautiful, cold fresh air, recommend it.'

'Good, that's good. I'm kind of working, have to go, but I'll call you.'

'No problem, son, play your best. Doesn't matter what level...'

'Play your best.'

Travis ends the call. His dad gave up the drink and the weed about ten years ago, but his mother had already left by then.

He continues searching the room. He finds a mobile on the top shelf of the closet and turns it on. Still heaps of battery life. No lock on it. He goes to contacts, only three numbers for Declan, Shaun, and Farez. Farez is a Lebanese or Moroccan name maybe. He calls Farez and waited. It starts ringing. Someone says, 'Billy, that you?'

Like maybe, you shouldn't be calling me now.

'Yeah, it's Billy.'

'You sound weird.'

'Cold. Want to catch up?'

'Since when do we catch up?'

'Oh, uh...'

'How do you know me, Billy?'

Travis ends the call.

Puts the mobile in the pocket of his jacket. He has to ask Ahn for Billy's mobile number. He wants also to know what happens when she rings Billy. Is it voicemail or does it ring out? Who are these three guys?

He calls her.

Ahn pickup. C'mon.

She answers.

'It's Travis. Do you know a Declan, Shaun, or Farez?'

'Declan is the bar manager at Billy's club.'

'Which makes me ask, what the fuck is happening with his club while he's missing?'

'Declan is running it. I call him every day. He's depositing the cash into a night safe on George Street at 7 am when the clubs closes. Everything looks good. Billy told me what he makes often enough.'

'Declan is a trusted guy then?'

'Yeah. Shaun and who?'

'Farez.'

'No, I don't know them?'

'Where'd you get these names?'

'Scraps of paper, notes left in Billy's bin.'

'Oh.'

'What happens when you call Billy's mobile?'

'Straight to voicemail, doesn't ring at all.'

'Talk later.'

Billy runs a retro 80's club in the city. Travis decides he'll have to go there tonight, if only briefly, to speak to Declan. He keeps searching the apartment but finds nothing else of interest. He'll use the speed tonight. He has his own weed. He wants to know where you would buy a Thai Buddha stick like that. He will check in with Gavin at the Cross, try to find out through him.

He has a couple of lines of the speed, a few vodkas, smokes a joint while watching St Kilda v Swans on Channel Seven. He finds it hard to watch sometimes. Guys who had been in his draft year were playing for both sides, but he loved the game too much to turn it off. The Swans win, a guy called Ahmed Salim kicks five for them from the half-forward flank. The guy was electric.

Travis puts the little baggy in his pocket along with the Buddha stick wrapped in some tissues. It is sticky as hell. He checks the back door, locks it. Angelo thought Travis was a cool dude, but he hadn't called back either about another time for the Chui meeting. Ahn working for Pete Rose and Angelo for Chui. A couple of old-style wheeler fucken dealers there. Premier makers; makers of MP's, like former tennis pro, John Anderson, who looks good and does what he is told. Chui and Rose are local council bribers, friends with benefits with the heads of powerful building unions, and they are the builders of shopping centres, apartment building complexes, and awful retirement homes. He knows Chui runs illegal gambling dens all over the city, and at all times both of them playing all sides and winning. Everyone knew it. Stuart Dunn, the president of his footy club, told him all about them one day when he'd had a few. Dunn was a couple of rungs below them, like Travis was now many rungs below the big time. They had each found their level; only Dunn was satisfied and Travis wasn't. This opportunity with Chui was all he wanted. A shot at the big time again, only in a different role now.

———

Angelo has been told by Andy Chui to set up the meeting with Travis tomorrow afternoon. Angelo wants to check a few things with Ahn, he calls her.

'Angelo.'

'Hi Ahn, I think I might have a job for Travis.'

'Cool.'

'I want to check a few things. Why'd you guys break up?'

'He likes the seedy side of life. He complains about it, but he delights in it.'

'And?'

'He's from a good family. Went to private school before he got kicked out. He could play football better than anybody. I used to love to watch him play, but I hardly do that ever now.'

'What happened?'

'You better ask him. You could Google it. Find out half-truths. My dad didn't approve of him. Travis was too wild. A footballer. Attention seeker, he called him. He did something. Something that ruined Travis' dream. You understand?'

'I think so. But he stayed with you?'

'I didn't do it, and he probably felt like if he had me, he won. At the time I wasn't even talking to dad. We came to Sydney to get away, but like I said, he swims in that sleazy, seedy world. I'm over it.'

'Anything else?'

'He's sexy. Some of my girlfriends couldn't understand what I saw in him; they still can't. But our bodies fitted each other; his shoulders, his hard stomach — and yeah, his cock, it was a perfect fit for me. He was hot. He knew how to make me come. Still does. How is that?'

Angelo coughs, runs his right hand through his hair, takes a breath.

'Probably not what I'm looking for, but...'

'He's a solid worker. He can find people if that's what you plan on him doing. Loyal too. He worked at that shithole in The Cross until yesterday, don't think he ever even took a day off. He still parties hard. Like I said, he swims with the sharks.'

'Are you taking your meds?'

'Yes, why?'

'You sound a little high.'

'Too much coffee, and you don't know me well enough to ask that.'

'What about you and your father?'

'He's my dad. An ogre, but my dad. I broke up with Travis, moved on, my dad got me my job, and I'm good at it. My dad says I can smell a rat.'

'And you found Billy.'

'Yes.'

'But he's missing.'

'Travis will find him.'

Angelo ends the call, calls Travis, who is about to leave the apartment.

'Angelo.'

'3 pm, tomorrow, at Mr Chiu's Potts Point apartment. I'll text you the address.'

'I thought he lived in Crow's Nest.'

'He owns a lot of property.'

'I'll be there.'

'I'm curious, Travis. What are doing at 11 pm on Friday?'

'I'm going to Billy's club. Ask a few questions of Declan, the night manager. Maybe dig around a bit. After that, it's my time.'

'No fear of the killer?'

'Mate, he saw me. He looked into my eyes. *My* eyes will be roaming the streets in front of and all-around me constantly, but I can't change my life. I have a few jobs to do now.'

'One other thing, Travis. Olsen rang me, told me there was CCTV last night outside the Cross Motel, but all they got was the back of a guy carrying a backpack on his left shoulder. It was hazy, couldn't even get the colour of his jacket.'

'Oh, great.'

'See you, Travis.'

'Yeah, bye.'

Travis walks out the door but decides finding Perry and Katya is more important than Billy. He's still going to Billy's club, but now he's walking fast along Victoria Street, to Kings Cross, to the dirty-half-mile for answers.

CHAPTER EIGHT

Travis walks into the Goldfish Bowl. It's the front bar of The Crest Hotel, that sits in the triangle where Victoria Street and Darlinghurst Road collide, then go their separate ways. He recognises a couple of faces. Goes and stands at the bar with them. Big Maori guy sticks his hand out, 'Travis, what's news brother? Been killing girls at your motel?'

Travis shakes his hand, says, 'Poor taste, even for you, big fella. The girl *is* dead.'

'Sorry, bro, you want a beer?'

'Yeah, schooner of New and a shot, Vodka. Think you can afford that, Tyrone?'

He doesn't get a bite. The other guy is Ted Janson. An ex-rugby league player. He also shakes hands with Travis, says, 'Saw the girl on TV. Ann something. She looked young.'

'She was. Hey, Ted, can you still buy weed in, um, put together like a Buddha stick, you know what I mean?'

'Oh, man. Haven't heard of that in a long time. You mean wrapped up to a stick with string and...'

'Yeah. You don't know any...'

'No, bro. You get one or you want one?'

'Mate of mine says he scored one here, down by the Piccolo Bar.'

Travis drinks his beer quickly, kills the vodka shot, presses their hands again, says goodbye, moves out the door onto the street proper, walks along in the direction of the Cross Motel but on the opposite side. He ducks down into the empty games parlour, now shooting gallery, where he smashed the chair through the office window. The Aboriginal boy isn't sitting on the orange stool in the office or anywhere else. A ragtag group of six or seven young people sit hanging out against the far wall. Travis walks over to them. Unwraps the stick from the tissue, shows it to them.

'Know where I can score one of these things.'

A few shakes of the head. One kid in torn jeans and a grey jacket with fur on the collar says, 'Why you asking us?'

'No reason. I want to score one or two.'

Silence for a few beats. The young people want him to leave, but he asks the same kid,

'You know the Aboriginal boy who was in here last night?'

'Yeah.'

'What's his name?'

'Paul.'

'Paul who?'

'Can't say.'

'Where can I find him? You saw me talking to him. I don't want to hurt him, nothing like that.'

'Enough questions. Fuck off, mate,' the kid in the jacket says.

Travis pulls a fifty note out of his pocket.

'This help your memory? And if you bullshit me I'll come back here and take it back.'

'He lives in a squat on Bourke Street, a three-storey terrace. Turn left off Williams Street, you'll find it.'

Kid puts his hand out. Travis hands him the note, says,' 'Remember, I'll come back, you got it.'

'You wait long enough there you'll find him.'

Travis knew Billy sometimes scored weed in The Cross. The last time he saw him, he had told Travis this because he thought it made him cool. Told him he went to the strip clubs sometimes, scored weed outside the Piccolo Bar. That was about a year ago. Billy showing off. That's what he does or did. How did Ahn's old man hate Travis and like Billy? Travis couldn't work it out. A dilemma never to be solved.

Travis turns and leaves, walks up the stairs out onto Darlinghurst Road again. It's buzzing. He walks along looking all around him. Neon signs advertising sex, bad taste souvenir shops with Australian flags hanging out the front. Cheap Thai cafés. He's looking for Katya or Perry or the Aboriginal kid. He walks past the railway station entrance. Some street kids, suburban boys and girls dressed up. A big Asian guy, a spruiker, grabs his arm while yelling, 'girls girls girls,' recognises him, says, 'Sorry, brother, you all look the same to me.'

Travis nods, smiles, keeps walking, walking to Katya's spot. She's not there. There's a café. He walks in, sits down at a stool facing the street. The café is open at the front. He could reach out, touch the throng as they walk by. He orders a Jack and coke, getting warmed up now, drinks it in gulps, crushing the ice. He's supposed to order food too, but they know him. He walks across the road, knocks loudly on the front door of the Cross Motel. Gavin sees him, smiles, probably thinks Travis wants more speed.

They sit in the back office, a side window open, smoking. Travis brings out the weed and shows it to Gavin.

'Know where I can score something like this?'

'Not from me, maybe, uh, no, never seen anything like it.'

'Is Bing working in the newsagent?'

'Yeah, you think he might know.'

'Maybe, he might be the only guy I know addicted to weed. He doesn't deal, but, um, give him a buzz, tell him to come in.'

The newsagent is next door. Gavin uses his mobile to text Bing; he texts him back almost instantaneously. *Be there in a sec.*

Gavin and Travis sit, and Gavin asks him, 'Cops giving you a hard time?'

'Yes and no. What did Mick say to you?'

'Plenty of extra shifts is what he asked for. I started at 5 pm going through to 7 am. Nice money I guess.'

'C'mon, about me?'

'You gave them the room for free or something. Didn't get them to sign a rego form.'

'You ever do that?'

'It may surprise you, but I like this job. I get my extras in dealing. Don't need to rip off the boss.'

Bing knocks on the front door, Gavin gets up, unlocks it, pulls it wide open. Bing grabs his forearm and squeezes, says, 'Alright?'

'Yeah, the man out the back wants to ask you something.'

Bing, Asian, skinny with a shaved head and rat's tails, walks out the back. Travis shows him the weed. Bing smiles, touches it, says, 'Man, that's sticky. It would be good to smoke, like, now. It's so pungent, the smell. C'mon, who cares where it came from, let's smoke up.'

Travis puts the stick back into the tissue paper, says, 'Another time, Bing. You see anything last night? You see the guy run out of here?'

'Sorry, nothing. I'm busy. I can't sit around like you guys. Gotta lock the door, put up a sign to sneak in here for a coffee or something. Even Monday, Tuesday 5 am, someone wants a newspaper, a sim card a fucken top up on their Opal card. '

'I have to go, Bing. Good to see you.'

'Be careful, Travis, that madman is out there still. Cops haven't got any idea. No CCTV, I hear. He disappeared like smoke.'

Travis leaves them, hits the street again, turns left down Roslyn. This'll be his last stop before heading to Billy's club. He sees a few small-time dealers. Twenty dollar weed deals. Half parsley leaves and basil to dope. He crosses over to the other side past a few cafés, still looking for Katya, Perry, the boy, someone, anything.

There's a small lane that runs off Roslyn Street behind where Barron's nightclub is. There are usually three guys pretending to sell weed, coke, speed, whatever you want, and they're here these guys. They tell newbies to follow them up the lane so they won't get seen by CCTV, then they roll them, bash them a little bit until they're too scared to report it. Travis knows them by sight, knows one guy by name, but he's not there. He signals to one of the guys, he comes down the lane, says, 'Back up this way, bro, away from the...'

'Don't want to score. I'm a friend of Katya, of Bodie.'

'Go see Katya, go see Bodie.'

'You know where they are?'

'Piss off, mate, I don't have time for this shit.'

Travis hasn't thought of Bodie until that moment. He works in a sex shop on Oxford Street, Darlinghurst. Katya, among other things, had told him he had the best cock she had ever seen, but she liked to talk hot like that, unsettle you. Bodie was a wild card. If Olsen looks dangerous, Bodie is. Travis had watched him one night when they all went drinking to the Aussie Rules Club. At the bar, this guy, a hanger-on, friend of Katya's, was ribbing him about working in the sex shop. Travis could see Bodie getting angry but not showing it, dialling it down, but he snapped at one point, grabbed the guy around the neck with one big paw, forced his head onto the rail running underneath the bar, smashed it into the bar. A bouncer, a big Islander, went to grab Bodie, and Bodie, he held off the Islander with one hand while still choking the hanger on until he was happy his point had been made. The Islander did nothing, was in a kind of shock that someone could ragdoll him like that. But Bodie is a job for another night. Hopefully, he can find Katya before that.

Travis crosses back over Roslyn Street. There are a couple of guys on the corner, outside the milk bar, Travis knows them by sight. He grabs one by the elbow, says, 'You know me, right?'

'Yeah, you're from the murder motel. They find the guy yet?'

'Don't know. Have you seen Katya or Perry?'

'No.'

He pulls out the tissue from his jacket, shows him the weed.

'What?'

'You sell this stuff? Like this I mean?' He shows it to him again.
'What the fuck is that?'
'OK, no, I'm guessing.'

Travis turns, walks quickly back the way he came, quickly but still searching for a face, maybe the killer, maybe someone who knows Katya, someone, anything. He turns left at Darlinghurst Road, walks past the spruikers yelling the same tired old shit. The pizza shops and dodgy bars and eateries, past girls selling their life away, old men up to who the fuck knows what? Maybe they're on their own. No family, no friends, looking for a connection to life, something to live for or they're old pervs. He feels like it's the same people, different night who wander up and down the street. He walks on a little further, a girl in tight jeans and a dirty black camisole asks him for a light. He pulls out his red Bic and lights her cigarette, she whispers to him, 'I'll give you a blow job for twenty bucks.'

Travis looks at her, she's attractive but roughed up. Still, he stirs for a few moments, the thought crosses his mind, but he rounds her quickly without looking back. He wonders how many guys say yes? How many times a night?

He reaches the taxi rank, jumps in a taxi, says to the driver, 'Angels night club.'

CHAPTER NINE

THE TAXI STOPS AT THE BEGINNING OF A SHORT LANE OFF PITT Street in the heart of the CBD. Travis walks past early leavers, joins the queue in a roped-off section outside the club. Red rope strung along silver poles like a million nightclubs all over the world. A tacky, sticky red carpet, laid out on the concrete leading to the solid wood front door. Angels written in a curving font in neon lights above the wood door.

Travis thinks, stuff this, walks to the front of the line, says to the girl checking ID, 'I'm a friend of Billy, need to see Declan.'

'I'm a friend of Billy's too, join the queue.'

Now he knows why they call them door bitches.

He goes back to the end of the queue; truth is it's not that long. A couple in front of him cling to each other like their lives depend on it, kissing, and the girl sneaking the odd groin rub in to make her boyfriend smile. People join in behind him. He listens to the conversations, switching between bored and intrigued. He gets through the wooden door only to be confronted by another queue to the cashier. He pays his $15 while listening to *Flock of Seagulls*. He enters the main room of the club, huge neon-lit dancefloor packed with people now dancing to *Everybody Wants to Rule the World*. He smiles, everyone knows this music no matter what age they are. It's why the club prints money, at least according to Ahn. Travis likes the music his old man listens to. Springsteen. Velvet Underground. Hoodoo Gurus. Van Morrison. Tom Waits. Like that.

He walks around the dance floor and up a couple of levels above it trying to find someone who looks like they run the place. He gives up quickly, goes to the bar, asks a barman wearing a white *choose life* T-shirt, 'Where can I find, Declan?'

'End of the bar,' he says pointing to a tall guy with Billy Idol blonde hair.

Travis pushes through the crowd watching Declan talk animatedly to a barmaid also in a *choose life* T. Declan is in all black clothing. Travis reaches them waves his hand in front of Declan's face who grabs it, starts bending it back until Travis reaches over the bar with his left hand and slaps Declan's hand way. Now, he has his attention, he says loudly and quickly before Declan can react, 'I'm a friend of Ahn and Billy. She hired me to find him. Travis Whyte.'

'Oh, yeah,' he yells back, 'she told me you were coming.'

'Somewhere we can go?'

'Outside. Follow me.'

He follows Declan back the way he came, then out past the cashier, out the front door.

When they're outside, clear of the queue, Declan turns to him, says, 'Don't ever fucken touch me like that again, especially not in front of my staff, you hear me?'

Travis backs away, dials down his anger, says, 'Alright, alright. Now, where's Billy?'

'No idea.'

'Who is Shaun? Who is Farez?'

Travis sees him blink rapidly, look down. He's going to lie but then shrugs, says nothing.

'Why would Billy have a phone with only three contact names in it?'

'I'm guessing me, and two other people, right?'

'Did Ahn mention to you that you should co-operate with me.'

'Or what?'

Travis sticks his right hand straight in Declan's throat, pushes him back at pace, out of the line of sight of the door bitch and bouncers up against a dirty brick wall, says, 'You start answering my questions or I will rip your throat out.'

Travis, shorter, much stronger, looking up at him, waiting, Declan nods. Travis takes his hand off his throat, says, 'Who is Shaun? Who is Farez?'

'Shaun used to work here. Don't know Farez. Never heard of him.'

'What did Shaun do?'

'Barman.'

'How long for?'

'A year, maybe longer.'

'Why'd he leave?'

'Sacked him.'

'Why?'

'Tried to hit on me and Billy, hit on other guys and…'

'Par for the course for a club, isn't it? Or wait, you don't like gays, or don't like them hitting on you. Freaks you out, makes you uncomfortable, right?'

'It wasn't only me. Billy canned him.'

'Farez?'

'Never heard of him.'

'I find out you do know him, I'll be back. Now, where can I find Shaun?'

'Give me your mobile number. I'll text you his, alright?'

'Alright, what time do you wake up tomorrow?'

'None of your business.'

'I have your number now too if I need you, anyway.'

'I have work to do.'

'Go work,' Travis says walking away down the lane, out onto Pitt Street, he finds a taxi straight away, says, 'Corner of Bourke and William Street, Darlinghurst. The taxi pulls away from the curb slowly and then the driver accelerates fast and hard and Travis thinks, my kind of driver.

CHAPTER TEN

He gets out at the Boulevard Hotel. It always reminds him of the James Dean poster, *Boulevard of Broken Dreams*. He crosses always-busy William Street, zigging and zagging through the cars, enjoying it stupidly. He turns into Bourke Street; there it is about ten houses along. Small chaotic front-yard full of weeds, an old rusted bike, the front porch is rotted wood. The windows above the porch boarded up. He tries the wooden front door, doesn't budge. Goes to the first window hoping his foot doesn't go through the porch. The board in the window swings open like it's on hinges. He sticks his head through. Dark, a bitter smell, like bad BO or piss or something. There are three mattresses on the floor. One occupied by someone in a sleeping bag, snoring. Not the Aboriginal boy, too big.

He climbs through the window, walks around the mattresses, through an open doorway into the hallway. A set of stairs before him. He walks straight down the hallway into a kitchen. Opens the pantry door. It's well-stocked with two-minute noodles, cans of soup, creamed corn, and pasta meals in vacuum packs. Someone's organised. There is a gas stove, a Nespresso coffee machine. Squatters do

OK these days. The fridge works, but there's only one two-litre plastic bottle of milk.

He takes the stairs to the first landing, checks the time on his phone. 1.30 am. There is a lounge room with a TV. Not huge but not small. A guy with a wispy beard asleep on the couch. Two torn up, black lounge chairs. The brown shag carpet encrusted with years of god knows what kind of shit. Never seen a vacuum. He moves out of the lounge, a closed door opposite. He decides to keep moving, come back to that one later. He starts walking up to the third floor, half-way up a voice says, 'Took your time, footballer.'

'Paul?'

'You got my name now brother, you one of the family,' he says laughing to himself, 'you gotta provide for me, bro,' he says still smiling.

'Got time to talk?'

'I look busy?'

'No.'

'Come up, I'm in the highest room.'

He follows the boy up the stairs around a corner, up a ladder to a small loft room. No bed, only bedding on the floor, a clothes rack, a chest-of-drawers. Travis turns, looks out the window. A million-dollar view of the city skyline, a glimpse of the harbour.

'You picked a good room.'

'Didn't pick nothing, had to fight for it, bro.'

'I need to know where Perry is?'

'You shoulda come to me first, footballer.'

'My name's Travis. Why is that?'

'They gone to Melbourne. Too hot for them here.'

'Who is they?'

'Perry and your girl, Katya. Perry asked me to come too. He got a car from somewhere, came around here this morning, about 11 am. Dragging me out of my bedclothes, asking me.'

'Katya?'

'I looked out the window, she was standing by the car, smoking.'

'What type of car?'
'Blue Celica, about ten years old I reckon.'
'Fuck that bitch. Fuck Perry. I... fuck!'
'You OK?'
'Perry tell you where he got the car?'
'Yeah. Car dealer in Surrey Hills. Near the Cricketer's Arms Hotel. That same street, anyway.'
'You sure about this?'
'Sure, no more questions now. I've been waiting for you. My friend Teddy said you were coming, probably. I need to sleep.'
'I'm playing on Sunday, 2 pm at Randwick, the ground is...'
'I know where it is. Might come too, Travis.'
'Hope you do, Paul. They have an under 19 team.'
'Good, see you, bro. I'm tired.'

Travis makes his way down the ladder and the stairs, back out the window. Finally, he thinks to himself, it's my time.

He walks across William Street, up to The Cross as it starts to rain lightly.

CHAPTER ELEVEN

He walks down the stairs into the Kardomah Café. The Commotions are playing a set of jangly guitar pop, and he likes it. The lead singer looks like Nico and is in a sliver miniskirt singing like an angel. Travis goes to the bar, almost immediately he sees a blond girl. Short blond hair like Katya's but not Katya. She is Lebanese, Greek or from Cyprus or somewhere exotic he decides, then laughs to himself cos he hasn't got a clue. He gets a double vodka from the bar and a beer. Nurses the drinks while following the girl, she turns for s second, a cherubic face, with a biggish round nose, soft features, thick eyebrows, the tiniest wisps of hair on her neck. He keeps following her, she nudges her dark-haired friend, they start dancing slowly together. Travis is mesmerised.

The band stops, and the hot singer in the silver mini whispers, 'Back soon, don't go anywhere.'

The exotic girl turns, stares straight into his eyes, he says, 'Hi.'

'What?'

'I'm Travis.'

'Oh.'

'Yeah, I...'

'I saw you looking at me, following me up here.'
'You're beautiful.'
'Oh my, a charmer.'

Travis laughs, says, 'The same question you get asked every day of your life. Where are you from?'

'At least you kinda jazzed it up, made it slightly different.'
'And?'
'Morocco.'
'Cool.'
'Been there?'
'No, but on the list.'
'Where have you been?'

'Mostly, Asia. Japan. Thailand. Vietnam. Laos. Cambodia. Taipei. Like that.'

'You like the band?'
'Love the band. Let's get another drink before they start again.'
'Alright.'

She tugs the sleeve of her girlfriend, points to Travis, says, 'Travis is buying me a drink.'

The girl laughs and the blonde turns back to Travis, says,' 'Let's go.'

'What's your name?'
'Babus.'
'I like it, it's cool.'

They walk down the back through a jam of people, Travis nudges his way through until they reach the bar at the back of the room. He orders double vodka with ice and a beer for him, turns back to Babus, says, 'What're you drinking?'

'CC and coke.'

The drinks come, and they stand up the back unable to see the band now as they start their new set. Babus points to an empty table, they climb up, stand on the table. Babus with her back against the wall. Travis standing beside her. They yell stuff at each other and laugh. The attraction is instant, and they press close against each other. Travis turns to her, she leans in straight away, kisses him on the mouth, he kisses her back, pushing his tongue slowly into her mouth, she responds in kind, runs her hand along his hip slowly, then quicker, it turns him on, makes him feel attractive, wanted. The band plays on. She manoeuvres Travis in front of her, wraps her hands around his stomach from behind, kisses his ear and neck, he leans back into her, she puts her hand in his left jeans pocket, leaves it there as he gets harder and harder. Both of them can see people are watching them but they don't care.

They stay that way through the set, Travis feeling hotter and hotter. When the band stops, he pulls away from her, but turns back, faces her and she puts her hand on his hip again holds him tight, he says, 'Let's get out of here.'

'Sure, I live not far away.'

'You're a Kings Cross girl?'

'No, Potts Point. Same thing, I guess. It's about a seven to ten-minute walk.'

'What about your friend?'

'She's a big girl.'

They climb down off the table, Travis takes her hand, leads her through the crush of people up the stairs out onto the street. When they hit the street, a flash of memory hits Travis. The girl, Ann, he is holding her hand as she bleeds out all over the sheets. Where was the killer? He calms down quickly. Babus not noticing anything. They lean against a steel railing outside the Kardomah, kiss again but separate quickly. She takes his hand now, leads him along Ward Ave to Roslyn Street up to Darlinghurst Road where Travis started his night and along to MacLeay Street. The crowd thinning out the farther they walk. Her building is a ten-storey apartment block that looks pretty Ritzy to Travis. They walk in, take the lift, kissing and pressing their bodies together, get out on the tenth floor laughing now. She guides him along the hall to her door. She presses the code, and the door opens. He glimpses a bright city view and she drags him through the apartment to the bedroom.

He kisses her again at the foot of the bed, she falls back grabbing him by the belt, sits on the edge of the bed facing him. She pulls at the belt, ripping it off, opening his jeans up, putting her hand inside his briefs, feeling him hard. Travis laughs, she says, 'What?'

'Nothing.'

His pants come down, she leans forward taking him in her mouth and the show begins.

Travis wakes up at 11 am. Babus no longer in bed. He feels good. Hungover but not a headache, a mild foggy brain with happy, sexy thoughts in his head. His guts churning for food though. He wonders where she is. He locates his pants and underwear, puts them on sans shirt. The apartment is warm. He walks through into the lounge; she's watching Rage hosted by some guy in a red and black flannel shirt.

'Who's hosting?'

'I forget his name.'

The guy introduces Purple Sneakers by You Am I. Travis says, 'Nice choice, you like these guys?'

'Sort of, not this song.'

'Last night you said you weren't working or were between jobs, right?'

'Yeah.'

'How do you afford this place?'

'My big brother bought it for me.'

'Nice brother. What's he do?'

'He owns a couple of clubs. One in Kings Cross and another in the city, plus he does real-estate, and he exports fruit and vegetables to Japan.'

The guy on Rage wearing the flannel introduces Kylie Minogue doing that song where she's wearing the white Grace Jones rip-off dress, looking sexy as hell. Travis admires his wide choices in music. Babus says, 'Now, I like this,' and gets up from the floor, wraps her arms around his waist and Travis smiles, says, 'You were pretty amazing last night.'

'You too. You know first nights can be, um, a letdown sometimes with drink and everything but...'

'But?'

'But not with you, not this time.'

'What's your brother's name?'

'Farez.'

'What'd you say?'

'Farez. Farez Abadi. Have you heard of him?'

'No. That's an unusual name though. I... nothing. It's cool.'

'You're looking at me all weird.'

'What's the name of the Club in the city? I might know it.'

'Angels.'

'Oh, yeah I heard of that. Supposed to be good,'

'It better be. Now come with me,' she says, grabs his hand, leads him back to bed.

A couple of hours later, he's at the McDonald's on Darlinghurst Road eating a Quarter Pounder and fries, sucking a coke through a straw, followed by a cheeseburger and a hot apple pie with another large coke. Hungover no longer. His stomach full. Only now can he think clearly. Farez. Not such a big coincidence given the world's they live in. Babus said Farez lived in Coogee. Fucken Katya and Perry, skipping town. He knew what he had to do. For Ann and her mother. He has to tell Angelo that the two of them are in Melbourne All anonymous information. Travis only thought it might have been Perry. Another source had confirmed it was. Something like that. He has an hour until the Chui meeting. He will ring Angelo after that. He walks out of Maccas along Darlinghurst Road to the Crest Arcade, to the TAB.

CHAPTER TWELVE

Andy Chui's building is on Grantham Street off Macleay Street. It used to be an old motel and has a concierge. He isn't wearing lapels but a blue bespoke suit with a white shirt, a deep blue tie. He's tall with tanned brown skin, lithe and good looking in an old fashioned, Gary Cooper kind of way. He says to Travis, 'How can I help?'

'I have an appointment with Mr Chui.'

'I'll ring him, won't be long.'

The foyer is small, he sits on a black leather sofa. There are photographs of Kings Cross, Potts Point, and Woolloomooloo on the walls. He particularly likes a black and white shot of Darlinghurst Road at peak time, around 2 or 3 am. It's interesting to see the bright lights and neon subdued, the faces of people clear and edgy, no colourful clothing. Bleak.

The concierge tells him to take the lift to the penthouse, Travis looks at his name tag, says, 'Thanks, Vincent.'

Concierge nods in reply, and Travis gets into the lift, presses the button, and the lift shoots up quickly to the top floor. Travis gets out, and there's a door right in front of the lift. It opens, and a small, birdlike woman stands there. Her light brown hair up in a bun, she is Caucasian, about thirty, Travis thinks. With a little hook nose, brown eyes, and a cute smile.

'I'm Carrie, Mr Chui's personal assistant, please come in,' she says opening the door wide.

Travis walks slowly through the door, then down a small set of stairs into a sunken, enormous lounge area that flows out onto an enormous balcony looking out to the city and across the harbour to the bridge. It would be spectacular at night Travis thinks. There are three sofas similar to the one in the foyer but bigger, a couple of lounge chairs, a full bar and lots and lots of bookshelves, so full of books that some are stuffed in any which way. It's not what he thought it would be. It's relaxed. The books make it kind of personal because they're not stacked in an orderly fashion but like someone picks them up regularly and read small pieces from them before putting them back. Chui enters the room from a long hallway that is mostly hidden. He is dressed in black chinos, a black T-shirt. He says to Carrie, 'We'll be fine on our own Miss Kingston.'

'Yes, sir,' she says, 'enjoy your time here, Travis.'

Travis thanks her and she disappears down the hallway. Travis turns to Andy Chui who is wiry little fucker. He has guns too but not bunched up; his biceps are long and lean, like his body. His face is speckled with freckles across his nose, Asian eyes, small, and dead black. Andy Chui puts out his hand, saying as they shake hands, 'Travis, Angelo is impressed by you, welcome.'

'Thank you.'

'Take a seat at the bar. I'll do the honours.'

Travis smiles, they both walk to the bar. Chui walks around behind it and says, 'What's your pleasure, Mr Whyte?'

'Lemonade would be good.'

Andy Chui laughs. Travis notices his whole face come alive now, the eyes no longer dead but playful.

'Had a big night last night.'

'Lemonade it is for the private investigator.'

'Thanks, and look, let's get down to it. What am I doing here?'

'Angelo thinks you could be useful.'

'And.'

'I'll start you on $1500 a week, as a kind of retainer for your services.'

'Doing what?'

'I run a few gambling clubs. Poker, Black Jack, Roulette. Small and simple. You would be starting on the door, later on, you can learn to close up, check the money, work with the gaming boss. It's small. A couple of doormen, two barmen, two waitresses, two security on the floor plus the gaming manager, a dealer for the blackjack and roulette. You already know Kings Cross, the things that can happen.'

'How many days?'

'Start with two nights a week. Thursday and Friday. You can still play football on Sunday. It's important to keep in shape, work hard at things you enjoy. Starting next week. Plus, I have other jobs I can use you for. I would pay a little more for you to do these things. Some debt collection, a little intimidation perhaps, some people need a push.'

'I can do all that.'

'Good. The main thing outside of that is to keep your mouth shut, and I'm not talking about your friend Ahn, she knows the score but be discreet, her boss can play dirty.'

'But you think it's a handy thing I know her, right? Her boss and her old man.'

'It could come in handy, yes, as you say.'

Chui hands him his lemonade. Travis takes it and gulps it down, looks around the big lounge once more at all the books.

'Alright, let me know what to wear and...'

'Angelo will call you and give you details of a tailor. You'll get two black suits, two white shirts, a couple of black silk ties. It's important to make a good impression at the door, set the scene. You'll be paid in cash on Saturday morning after the club closes, which can be as late as 7 am.'

'Sounds good. I appreciate it.'

'You'll need a handgun too. Angelo will organise a license.'

'Ok, sure.'

'At night on the door of the clubs I own, you'll be able to assess people straight away. If you think they need to see the handgun, open your jacket enough so that they can see it. They should behave after that. Oh, one other thing, have you seen the news today, the newspapers?'

'No, why?'

'Detective Inspector Olsen is under suspicion of corruption for taking bribes when he was in the drug squad, using informants…'

'He was in the drug squad?'

'Yes. No charges yet, only rumour and innuendo.'

'I got the impression he was a pretty straight shooter.'

'That's what he wants you to think.'

'Right.'

'The door is open. Let yourself out. I'll call you when I need you. I have your mobile, know where you live so, no problem.'

Travis thinks Chui might have been saying, be careful, when he said he knew where he lives, or maybe it was Travis being paranoid. It sounded good. His whole world was about to change. Had changed with the killing of an innocent girl. He decides he will learn a lot working for Andy Chui. The money is good. Cash too. On the street, outside Chui's building, he takes his mobile out. He has to tell Angelo about Perry and Katya, it is the only thing to do, for the girl Ann and her mother, but he hesitates because it is Katya, puts the mobile back in his pocket. He hails a taxi on MacLeay Street back to Billy's place. He has the love letter signed by Jeffy to figure out. He should have asked Declan at the club if he knew the name. Stupid mistake. He has Shaun and Farez to find and talk to.

CHAPTER THIRTEEN

Travis wakes up at around six in the morning. He has slept almost from the time he arrived back at Billy's place. He checks his mobile. He has missed calls from Ahn, Angelo, and Katya. He rings Katya straight away. She might still be up from Saturday night somewhere.

'Travis.'

'You lied to me. You used me like you used me in the motel every second night you...'

'Hey, hey, hey. I'm talking to you now, Travis. I'm telling you where I am. I'm in Melbourne in an Airbnb in Abbotsford.'

'Right in the heart of smack city central on Victoria Street no doubt.'

'They have an injecting room like the one in The Cross.'

'Only surrounded by better cafes and those lovely Viet restaurants.'

'That's more like you, baby. Which is the best one? You like those Viet girls, don't you?'

'I have to tell them about Perry.'

'What about Perry? I rang you for the free room. You can't say it was Perry. You can't. Not me either. They'll crucify us. Hookers leading the killer to the girl. We wouldn't stand a chance.'

'You know the young Aboriginal boy that Perry likes?'

'No.'

'The one who Perry asked to come to Melbourne while you were waiting in the car you bought for your little trip. The one who says Perry told him about a guy, some guy who wanted to kill. A thrill kill.'

'That's crazy, baby. Crazy talk. That boy... he... he doesn't know anything.'

The call ends. She cut him off. He calls her straight back, but it goes straight to voicemail. He knows roughly where they are now. That is something.

He calls Olsen. It also goes to voicemail. Cops have to sleep sometime too. He gets up, walks naked down the hall to the toilet. Pisses a long steady stream, comes back to the second bedroom. Grabs a clean towel and hits the shower. He is going to call Angelo, tell him the story the Aboriginal boy told him about Perry. Tell him to call Olsen. Give Perry up. Tell him they were in Melbourne. Hanging around Victoria Street, Abbotsford. Katya could be lying through her teeth. They might be in Springvale or the Western Suburbs or holed up in some cheap motel in the northern suburbs. As long as Katya got her hits, she didn't care, but they'd need money. She might work for an escort agency or a parlour, she had done it before until Perry started pimping her on Darlo Road. She still looked good. The drugs preserving not destroying, although that was only a matter of time. Perry could swing both ways he assumed. The street sex worker scene unknown to them in Melbourne but everyone knew Grey Street, knew the small side streets off Carlisle Street.

He dries himself off, changes into black jeans, a light blue, long-sleeved shirt, put his favourite, scuffed, black leather jacket on. He feels like the cop in *The Friends of Eddie Coyle* when he wears it. Uncle would be happy. He chuckles to himself, walks out into the cold, damp, grey clouded day, heading to Victoria Street.

Travis is at the Tropicana Café. It is reliable and the coffee excellent. He finds a table against the window. It is quiet still. He drinks his strong flat white, watches the early morning and leftover people from the night before as they walk by him. Some still laughing. One doomed looking man in black, his face ashen. Travis wonders what happened to the doomed man. His girl dumped him. Kissed another man or another girl. He rips one of his croissants in half and stuffs some in his mouth.

He rings Declan, and while no-one is looking, dips some of the second croissant into his coffee, drops it into his mouth. Declan answers, Travis says, 'Who is Jeffy?'

'What? Oh, you're the cop from last night.'

'Not a cop, you know that. Who is he?'

'Jeff is like Shaun, he used to work here.'

'He was into Billy too.'

'Was he? Not to my knowledge.'

'You about to go home, Declan.'

'Soon. Why?'

'Any idea where Billy is? Last chance before I do tell the cops.'

'Oh man, you are painful, you know that.'

'I know.'

'Jeff's parents died and left him a holiday house on the Central Coast near Avalon. Maybe they're all down there fucking each other.'

'Maybe they are. Sounds like Billy to me.'

'Hey, you know what? Billy plays around, he fucks a lot of people, staff and other, but until he went missing in action, he turned this place into a goldmine. Six nights a week this place rocks, so fuck off, alright.'

Declan now with a set of balls hangs up on Travis.

Travis rings him straight back.

'Need the address of the place on the Central Coast. Phone number if you got it.'

'I'll text it to you.'

Travis calls Billy's mobile. It goes straight to voicemail again. Thing is. Billy trusts Declan and so does Ahn. Billy then might figure if he goes partying for a while that everything will still run smoothly, even if only for a month or so. Did Ahn give him a reason to act like this? Did she fuck someone else? Travis gets up from the table, buys a takeaway strong coffee at the counter, walks back down to Billy's place.

Inside he lights a cigarette. Shaun and Jeff are the keys here to finding Billy. Like Katya and Perry were the key to finding the killer. Farez? Travis thinks that Billy started to dabble again in dealing and Farez was his man. He rings Babus, she answers sleepily, 'Hello, lover.'

'Babus, hey. Do you know a guy called Billy Madison?'

'Who? What?'

'His name is Billy Madison. He knows your brother, Farez.'

'You're telling me you know Farez?'

'I don't know him, but his mobile number was in a contact list in a mobile that belongs to Billy. He and I go back a bit and the thing is he's missing. I've been hired to find him.'

'I don't know the name.'

'Do you think that you could put me together with your brother, Farez?'

'Did you know who I was Friday night? Did you come onto me to get to my brother?'

'No.'

'OK, I don't know, yet. Why don't you come over here, and we can talk about it?'

He heard the heat in her voice. They weren't going to be talking much and he played better after sex.

'I'll be there in half-an-hour, but I gotta play football this afternoon.'

'Can I watch?'

'Sure, why not.'

———

Babus gets out of the shower naked, walks into the bedroom, across to the walk-in closet. She chooses blue jeans, a white t-shirt, a blue jumper with threads hanging off the wrist and holes in the elbows, throws them on the bed next to Travis. He is also naked, smoking a cigarette, says, 'I'm so glad you smoke.'

'Planning on being around me, are you?' She says, choosing white bra and red panties from her chest-of-drawers on the other side of the bed to where Travis sits up straight now saying, 'I would like to.'

'Yeah, me too. Don't know why yet, but I like you.'

Travis stubs the cigarette out in the ashtray on the floor, jumps up, puts on his underwear and jeans, walks around the bed as Babus gets dressed, says, 'I have to fly. Need to get my kit from home and head to the ground. You still thinking of coming.'

'Yep.'

'I'll see you there,' he says, grabbing her around the waist, and she laughs and drops her bra, and he pushes her back onto the bed and she says,

'Yes.'

Travis knows he will give up smoking when he turns thirty, younger than his old man, but he smokes easily twenty a day now. Thirty or forty if he goes out partying like with Babus. He's driving the Triumph and it's purring at the last set of traffic lights before he reaches the oval. He'd like to see Paul on the boundary line. Another person he can't let the cops know about. He still hasn't rung Angelo. He has to tell him about Perry. The lights change, he drives into the footy ground gravel car park, takes his mobile out and calls Angelo, who answers, and Travis tells him about what the Aboriginal boy said about Perry, about knowing someone who was talking about killing a girl, that Perry was in Melbourne.

But he didn't tell him the full truth. He said it was a young rent boy from the wall who had been in the shooting gallery when he went looking for Katya. He kept Katya's name out of it. But mentioned Perry by name and that he was in Melbourne, hanging around on Victoria Street, maybe using the free injection room. He tells Angelo to tell Olsen all this. Angelo tells him he will, that he will tell Olsen the young rent boy had volunteered the information in the shooting gallery but not on the night of the murder, two days later, last night. That's all he knew.

It liberated Travis; he would play out of his skin today. Free of the burden and keeping the boy and Katya out of it. He enters the change rooms full of bravado, greets his teammates with handshakes and high fives, telling them that they will crush Maroubra today.

CHAPTER FOURTEEN

AT THREE-QUARTER TIME TRAVIS HAS THIRTY POSSESSIONS AND three goals, but the game is close. Maroubra is hard at it. They play an uncompromising, brutal style, and some of the younger Randwick players are feeling it. An elbow in the back of the head or their big ruckman 'accidentally' falls on some of the smaller players after ruck contests. They jumper punch and scrag and the umpire is a wimp. Travis looks up from the three-quarter time huddle, sees Paul at the far end of the ground behind the railing at the back of the goalposts. He is standing near Babus. Both there to watch Travis, but not knowing the connection. The coach finishes his address and Travis draws the group around him, and he grabs the jumper of the Randwick ruckman and screams at him.

'You protect the small blokes. You fucken get into their ruckman. I mean it. You go out and fucken belt him. The umpire won't do shit. Make a statement. You two, Mick and Anton,' he says, pointing to the big back man and the main forward, 'stand tall for your fucken teammates. Now, let's win this game!'

Randwick win by ten points. Their ruckman belted the other

ruckman, and it worked. Randwick won and Travis ended up with four goals and was best on ground.

He runs down to the goal square at the end of the game, feeling relief, a kind of joy he only gets from winning games of football. Babus smiles at him, saying, 'You were pretty good. A grade above most of them I think.'

'Nah, all of them,' he says laughing. 'Hey did you see a young Aboriginal boy here earlier?'

'Yeah, um, he went up to the kiosk. There he is.'

Paul walks back towards them eating a pie and smiling.

'You can play a bit,' he says to Travis. 'This your girlfriend?'

'Friend,' Babus says and puts out her hand. 'I'm Babus.'

Paul smiles, not used to people being polite to him. He shakes her hand, says, 'That's a nice name. Where's that name from?'

'Morocco.'

'Morocco, hey. I'm going to google that on my phone.'

He takes the phone out of the back pocket of his long baggy shorts and Travis sees that it's new, that the kid's clothes are new, wonders what he had to do to get the money. Makes a mental note to ask the President about getting the kid a job at a carwash or supermarket, something away from whatever he does now.

'You two coming into the rooms. They let girls in now I hear,' Travis says.

'As long as you wear a towel,' Babus says, and Paul laughs. Travis says, 'Come on you guys.'

They all walk up to the change room. Travis breathes in and out deeply wanting to enjoy the win, enjoy being with these two people. He'll ask the under 19 coach about getting Paul down to training.

Travis showers, re-emerges, gets back slaps and high fives and is generally treated like royalty. Randwick knows how lucky they are to have a player like him. He dresses and finds the under 19 coach, takes his arm, drags him over to meet Paul and Babus. Travis says, 'These are my friends, Babus and Paul. Paul wants to come and train with you. That be alright?'

'Yeah, no worries. Always after players. Paul, have you played before?'

'Yeah, I grew up around Albury Wodonga, played some juniors there when I was younger. I'm seventeen, now, look younger cos I'm small, but I'm fast, good kick at goal.'

'Alright then. We train on Tuesday and Thursday at 5.30 pm under lights. That be alright?'

Travis says, 'I'll bring him to the ground.' He says looking at Paul, 'take him home too. That alright, Paul?'

'Yeah, that's cool.'

The coach wanders away, Travis says to Paul, 'You want a lift home now? I'm taking Babus home, it's no problem.'

'Yeah, thanks, Travis,' he says using his name for the first time. 'You big time around here.'

They walk to Travis' car, and he turns the key in the ignition but his mobile rings. He says, 'One-second guys,' and answers the phone.

A voice says, 'Travis Whyte?'

'Yeah, Olsen. What now?'

'That is Mr Olsen or sir to you, Travis, got that?'

'Yeah, I got it.'

'You and your fucken lawyer think you got things cosied up now. An anonymous prick rings you up, tells you where this cunt Perry is and you're off the hook and...'

'Hey, I hear you aren't so nice and shiny anymore either.'

'You fucken little prick. I will get you for obstructing justice, that's for starters then...'

'Talk to my lawyer. He'll be glad to answer your questions.'

Travis ends the call.

Shit.

He starts the car again. His day fucked up.

He drops Paul at the squat. Takes Babus to her place, parks out the front, she says, 'You're a great player. I mean, like, wow, I was shocked. I don't know much about AFL, but I know you're amazing...'

'I'll tell you a story about it one day. About what might have been.'

She looks at him differently for a few seconds. A past he wants to talk about.

He turns towards her, says, 'Meeting you the other night. Um. Things seemed to have moved quickly.'

'Is that good or bad.'

He leans in, kisses her cheek, says, 'Oh, it's good. Definitely good.'

'Because you get to meet my brother.'

'That and the sex is pretty wild too.'

'Oh, yeah, there is that too.'

They kiss passionately for a few minutes. Babus puts her hand to his face as they draw apart and says, 'Such a good-looking man.'

'Such an exotic woman.'

'Thank you.'

'Yeah, totally different to anyone I've met or been with before, but I have to go now. I'm working on this case I told you about. I got a new job too. I have to drive up to the central coast.'

She bows her head slightly, hiding a bit of disappointment, says, 'Yeah, and what's with Paul? Is he, um. I don't know. Are you helping him?'

'That's another story. I'll tell you when I get back from the coast, but yeah, gotta move, babe. Gotta go.'

She gets out of the car and walks away without turning back. He drives off up Macleay Street towards Kings Cross.

CHAPTER FIFTEEN

Travis walks up the steps from Lamrock avenue to his apartment. Walks down the side of the building along the fence, opens the screen door, the front door. He throws his football kit on the floor of the lounge room and goes into the kitchen. He won't be going to the central coast until tomorrow.

There's a knock on the door. Travis hesitates. Did someone follow him? No one turns up here unannounced. They ring first. It's something he insists on from people. Did Babus ring Farez, tell him about them? Is it the killer come to take out the only witness? He doesn't have a fisheye. He opens the door slightly, sees a tough-looking, stocky man, short back and sides haircut, dressed in a suit, white open neck shirt. Cop? Did he lock the screen door?

He opens the front door a bit wider as the man opens the screen door more. Travis says, 'Can I help you?'

The man opens the screen door wide.

'I'm a cop. Olsen sent me to bring you in.'

'Got ID?'

'Sure,' he says, opens the right side of his jacket. Travis follows the movement with his eyes and the guy says, 'I'm a different kind of cop,' and bends his knees, throws a ripping left hook hitting Travis under the ribcage.

'Oomph.'

Travis has the wind knocked out of him, maybe even a busted rib. He goes low to protect himself, but the guy grabs him by the hair. Travis charges head down. The guy rips some hair out but drops his grip. Travis bulldozes him into the screen door, the guy trips and falls backwards. Travis lifts his right foot, smashes it into the guys' teeth with his Doc Martens. The guy takes it, rolls away fast, tries to get up, Travis lifts his foot again. The heavy black shoes raised, but the guy manages to roll quickly away but this time keeps going, gets up, runs away down the side passage. Travis doesn't follow him. Good fucken riddance. But he's pissed. His apartment is sacred to him, and this guy, this *different kind of cop*, has breached the walls, almost. Who the fuck was he?

He changes the setting on his phone to hide his number, calls Olsen, 'DI Olsen.'

'I just saw off your little ball of muscle.'

'Don't know what you're talking about Travis.'

'You *are* bent *aren't* you.'

'Do you have some information concerning the death of Ann Gables, Mr Whyte.'

'No.'

'Your time is coming, Travis.'

'Good to know.'

Travis ends the call. Olsen did send him. That little ball of muscle. Travis got lucky, he had him down, the guy was right to run. No point getting your head stomped on. But it played on his mind. Brought back memories of the night he looked into the killer's eyes because he was *still* out there too. He wanted to ask Olsen what he'd done with the information about Perry, but that was impossible now. He had made another enemy, but he also had found a friend, maybe a mentor, in Andy Chui.

It is 6.30. Dark outside. He is exhausted. He cooks himself a pasta meal with some dubious looking mushrooms, some basil pasta sauce bought in a bottle, still hanging in there on the use-by date. He wishes he had crusty bread, some red wine. A joint. Ah, he did have a joint, he remembered. He had the sticky buddha stick he found at Billy's place. It was in his kit bag. He laughed out loud he was so happy about it. He took a piece of the sticky dope, crushed it up in his hand, resin sticking to his fingers, added a half-a-cigarette, expertly rolled it up. Put some flame to it, breathed in deeply. Felt the strength of the dope almost straight away, the smell of it getting him high too, it was pungent as hell. He blew the smoke out smiling. He would sleep tonight despite everything going on. Grass always allows him a good night's sleep. He hopes it continues that way.

CHAPTER SIXTEEN

Travis wakes up at six on the dot, staring at the bright red numbers on his clock radio. He had been dreaming about Perry and Katya. He had seen them together at a club somewhere laughing and dancing. He was looking down on them from a balcony, getting angrier and angrier as he thought of Ann slashed to pieces while these two danced and laughed the night away. Then he woke up. He didn't know what was worse. Seeing the girl cut to pieces or Katya and Perry dancing and laughing. Katya can't have known what was going to happen. He knows her. He spoke to her nearly every night for a couple of years. He has to find a way to get past it.

An hour later he is driving over the Bridge lighting a cigarette from the car cigarette lighter, the hot burning red end taking some tobacco with it when he slotted it back in its hole, creating an awful stink for a second or two. He opens the little triangular side window with the little latch to flick the ash out. The old car is purring beautifully, he is looking forward to letting it out as the speed limit increases the further he goes.

His mind goes over the past four days like a film in fast forward. How have all these things happened and still he played football yesterday as though nothing had happened? He is surprised by the lack of passion at the club about the murder. No outrage, more like gossip. What happened? You were there? Society is used to these vicious killings, but he had been there at the centre of it.

He has a job to do. Ahn or her father is paying him to find Billy. He wonders if Declan sent him on a wild goose chase, but Travis has a feeling something isn't right with Shaun and Jeffy. One was sacked, another writes a love letter to Billy. Babus had told him Farez owned Angels nightclub, but Ahn said all the banking deposits were correct. He took his mobile from the inside of his black leather jacket, pressed the button on Ahn's name. She answered quickly, he put it on speaker then put it in his shirt top pocket while he drove, saying to her, 'Listen, Ahn, I mentioned Farez to you the other day.'

'Yeah.'

'I spoke to his sister. She said that Farez owns a nightclub in the city called Angels.'

'I... shit. It's not true. I told you. I don't know that name.'

'Could it be true? Could Billy have done some deal with this Farez that you do...'

'Travis, we're talking about Billy. Anything's possible, but Billy would have to be... his name isn't on any paperwork.'

'You say Declan's deposits in the night safe are on target.'

'Yeah, Billy used to do the books each morning, well, each day, usually when I got home from work. He was kind of training me, you know, this is what we make on a Saturday night compared to a Monday night, later he would get the point-of-sale dockets from the club and come back and he'd show me. By showing me all this he was telling me he had his shit together. He was making extraordinary money.'

'Right, right.'

'Where are you, it sounds like wind blowing or something?'

'I'm driving to the central coast. To Avalon. I have to tell you a couple of other important things.'

'Alright.'

'At Billy's place, I found a love letter to him from a man named Jeffy. I also found a mobile phone with three numbers in it. Declan, Shaun, and Farez. I told you about Farez, you know about Declan. Declan told me he sacked Shaun, he also told me Shaun and Jeffy know each other. That Shaun has a house at Avalon. You connecting the dots?'

'Yes, what kind of love letter?'

'How many kinds are there?'

'Was it, I...'

'Be prepared for anything is what I'm saying. I'm going to meet Farez when I come back. You're paying me. I'm telling you the score. It's my job.'

'Thanks, Travis.'

'You alright?'

'Can you come and see me as soon as you come back?'

'Yeah, first thing, but from Wednesday through to Sunday I can only call you. I'll be too busy, but I'll come straight to you when I get back from Avalon.'

'Bye.'

Travis is well past the Bridge, onto clean road now. He accelerates while searching the pile of tapes he has dumped on the passenger seat. He finds Richard Clapton, his dad's all-time favourite, pushes it into the ancient cassette deck of the Millennium Falcon and in that unmistakeably gravel voice Clapton starts singing Deep Water.

An hour-fifteen later, Travis parks on the beachfront at Avalon opposite the Peppers Resort, sits on the grass. Shaun, Jeffy, and maybe Billy were only five minutes away if Declan has been straight with him. He lights a cigarette, looks out across the flat, deep blue ocean, a gun-metal sky overhead. It is peaceful. He wonders if he might live in a small place like this one day. Away from the traffic and the wonderland that is Kings Cross and in some ways the whole of Sydney. Thrill killers, bent cops, cheating scheming prostitutes, predators like Perry who do anything for money and good times, and soon he'll be immersed in it, even more, working for Andy Chui.

He quickly gets back into the car, drives to the address he has. It is a small circuit street. Travis parks outside the wooden house. It is painted a chocolate brown colour, has a small white picket fence. He reaches over behind the passenger seat, finds his gun. He has taken it from the safe he had installed under the floorboards, under his bed. He knows that Farez is probably a drug dealer, that he has some hold over Billy. *Since when do we catch up.* The tone of his voice had sounded defiant to Travis, like, *what the fuck are you calling me for? We have a deal?* He opens the steel, slightly rusted, gate. The wind picks up, huge drops of rain start to fall from the sky as he makes it under the small balcony. He can hear music, some kind of dance music, loud, he doesn't recognise it. All he hears is a continuous low thump of bass and rhythm. He knocks loudly on the front door instead of using the bell and waits. Knocks loudly again, the door is flung open by a small man with dyed blond hair wearing a floral apron with no shirt on and skinny hairless legs sticking out under the apron.

'There's a bell you know,' he says.

Travis gives him a cold hard look and the man backs slightly away. Travis walks in uninvited, the small man says, 'Hey, hey, I didn't ask y...'

'Are you Shaun or Jeff?'

'What?'

'You fucken heard me. Are you Shaun or Jeff?'

'I'm Shaun. Look I didn't ask you in and...'

'Ask me in, then.'

'Who are you?'

'Where's Billy?'

'What?'

'Who is it?' A voice yells from somewhere inside.

'I'm Travis,' he says to Shaun. Billy's girlfriend hired me to find him. You know Billy who sacked you, who owns Angels nightclub?'

'He's not here.'

'Let's walk into the lounge or the kitchen, shall we? Where your friend Jeff — or is it Jeffy — is.'

'Alright, alright, come in. I met Ahn once, she's lovely but...'

'Oh, you met her, did you.'

'Yes I...'

'Keep walking.'

Travis follows Shaun into the lounge. Jeff is bald and lying on the couch naked. His cock lying limp in his black pubes. He doesn't bother to cover himself when Travis walks in.

Shaun says, 'Jeff, this is Travis, he's looking for Billy.'

Jeff says, 'What the fuck?' And smiles.

'You heard him, Jeff, I'm looking for Billy.'

Jeff blinks a few times, still not bothering to cover himself at all. The music beats on annoying Travis. The TV is on with the sound down. A porno is playing, men and women on screen, not a gay porno. Travis recognises the Hedgehog, hides a smile. The black curtains on the windows are closed. An obese, blond Labrador sits in the middle of the room not moving, breathing heavily. Travis looks straight at Jeff says, 'I read your little love letter to Billy.'

'You what?'

'Put some shorts or jeans on, now!'

Jeff gets up quickly, rushes out of the room. Travis turns to Shaun says, 'Turn the music off. Turn the TV off.'

'How dare you speak to us like this in our own home and...'

'Do it.'

Shaun starts giggling again irking Travis and says, 'I will not put up with this. Get out! Get out of this house now.'

Travis pulls the gun out from the back waistband of his blue Levi's. Points it at Shaun says, 'Turn the TV and music off.'

Shaun turns the music and TV off.

Jeff comes back in wearing yellow shorts.

'When was the last time you saw Billy?' He asks both of them.

'He was here for a few days, but he's gone. Left two days ago,' Jeff says.

They both look at each other smiling.

Travis puts the gun down on a coffee table, sits in the hard-backed wooden chair next to it.

'Where'd he say he was going?'

'Back to Sydney,' Shaun says.

'To his house? To Ahn's place? To see Farez? You know Farez?'

'Back to Sydney,' Shaun says, 'that's all we know.'

'But you know Farez?'

They looked at each other, Shaun saying nothing. Both start laughing.

Travis getting more and more pissed off says, 'But you know Farez, right? The drug dealer. You know him or you fucked him or you did something for him. Am I right?'

'I know him,' Shaun says, 'we both do. We partied with him and Billy, but not just the three of us, a huge party he had in Coogee.'

'Billy's not here?'

'No, he's not here,' they both say at once and smile at each other and it makes Travis feel mad as hell.

Something fucked up is happening here.

'Why don't you both show me around?' Travis picks up the gun again.

He walks with them through the small house, through the kitchen, through two bedrooms, which he roughly searches for any clues to Billy's existence. Nothing. They open the back door. There is a granny flat and a Hills Hoist. Two short-sleeved blue shirts, two pairs of black jeans, a row of boxer shorts and t-shirts hung on it.

'What's in the granny flat?'

'Granny,' Shaun says and both men giggle, and it dawns on Travis that they are high, not ganja stoned, maybe tripping or even high on E. Yes, probably E to be smiling and giggling in this situation. Shaun and Jeff keep looking at each other and smiling. Travis wants to hit them both across the mouth, smarten them up, but he leaves it. He tries the door to the granny flat, but it is locked.

'Can you open this?'

'Why?'

'Why the fuck do you think I'm here? Get the keys.'

'I don't have them,' Shaun says. 'My mother never used the place, and we can't find the keys anywhere.'

'Get back inside,' Travis says.

Once inside he takes another, longer look around the bedrooms but can't find anything.

He comes back into the lounge after finding nothing.

'This is my mobile number,' Travis says, handing Shaun one of his PI business cards. 'You hear anything from Billy, you call me.'

'Yes, yes, we will,' Shaun says.

Travis opens the front door, walks down the short path, gets into his car. Stows the gun back under the passenger seat. Starts the car, drives out and along the small circuit, heads to another street at the back of the circuit to the back of the holiday house where the two of them still are.

Travis runs down the side passage of a house at the rear of Jeff and Shaun's place. No dog. No sign of anyone home. He jumps the fence into the holiday house of the stoned boys, his heart racing; he can't breathe for a second. Shit. Not this now. He puts his right hand over his chest, starts breathing in and out. He is on the ground now, on his knees, he keeps trying to suck in air. The back door opens, Shauna and Jeff walk out into the yard. Jeff says in a high-pitched voice,

'What the fuck are you doing? What's going on?'

They start laughing. Travis sucks in air, slowly gets his breath back, gets his anger back. He looks at the clothesline. The black jeans, the blue shirts, Billy's uniform. He always wore black stretch jeans. Always Levi's. He is angry now. Gets up and charges the granny flat door. Knocks it off its rusty hinges, bursts in and there is Billy, on a camp bed. Tied down by cables. Track marks in the crook of his left arm. Two syringes on a small plate beside the bed. Then the stench hits Travis. He touches Billy's left arm. Cold, hard, stiff. The two men are running to a car on the street when Travis catches up to them. He tackles Shaun to the ground and holds him there. Jeff makes it to the small red Hyundai, starts the engine. Travis is trying to hold Shaun who is bucking and yelling out and the car drives off leaving them both lying on the road.

The police arrive. Travis tells them his story. They interview Shaun and catch up with Jeffy twenty kilometres out from Avalon on the highway to Sydney. Not the smartest move. The cops clear Travis quickly. He drives to the police station, waits. After Shaun is interviewed, one of the constables comes out and tells him that Shaun and Jeffy did it for revenge, for dumping both of them. That they loved him. They lured Billy there with a story of one last party. They had the last party but after that doped him, tied him up, shot him full of heroin. Travis rings Ahn, tells her the story straight, she gulps back tears.

Travis says, 'I'm coming straight back for you. Don't go anywhere, ring me if you want to talk, but wait there for me.'

CHAPTER SEVENTEEN

LIKE IN TRAVIS' DREAM, KATYA AND PERRY ARE DANCING together in a cavernous nightclub in Melbourne in a laneway off King Street. Katya is wearing tight black satin pants, a tight purple crop top, that shows off her tight stomach, long sleeves that hide her heroin tracks. Perry is in a long black skirt, sky-blue blouse; his green eyes shine bright. His hair is short like Audrey Hepburn in Breakfast at Tiffany's. They both dance hard to a thumping bass beat. Katya is high and has added speed to the mix too. Perry is straight, strong-willed, only takes heroin very occasionally, never with a needle. He is still flush with cash from Sydney and is paying for everything including the Airbnb in Abbotsford.

A Greek guy slides up beside Perry, starts mimicking his dance moves, Perry likes it, he's going to play with this fucker, yes he is. His friend, another Greek boy, younger, starts dancing with Katya, she smiles at him, he smiles back, takes her from behind around the waist. Katya turns, looks over her right shoulder at her new man, smiles again, then bursts away from him spinning and laughing. The young guy follows her, grabs her again, she leans into him, kisses him on the neck, the young man laughs, and they all keep dancing.

Later, the four of them are in the female toilets. Katya is bent over the closed toilet seat snorting a line of speed, her young man is holding her hair back from her face. Perry and the older Greek guy are kissing in another cubicle and the man reaches under Perry's skirt, but she pushes him away, not yet, he's not ready, they kiss some more, then do a few lines of speed each.

They all walk out of the female bathroom and Perry says,

'Let's go back to our place, now, c'mon.'

The two men look at each other and laugh. Katya laughs too and says, 'I'm ready,'

The two men smile at each other. They all hit the street, Perry calls an Uber and as they climb in Perry says to the driver, 'Everything all right.'

'Everything's fine madam,' the driver says, and Katya laughs, the Uber takes them up and onto Victoria Parade, straight over Punt Road, along bustling, hustling Victoria Street, where junkies walk with high-end restaurateurs. There are low rent, cheap take-away food places, massage bars, too many bakeries and over Church Street, they go, a few hundred metres later turning into a little side street on the right. They all clamber out.

Perry says loudly, 'Let the festivities begin,' and looks at Katya and they laugh.

Inside, it's a two-bedroom apartment among ten or twelve other apartments in the same block, there is music and loud TV noise from the apartments all-around them. The men collapse into big brown armchairs.

Katya says in a sing-song voice, 'I'll get the drinks.'

Perry says, 'Me too.'

There are Vodka and soft drinks in the fridge. Katya goes to work getting ice from the freezer and the two of them mix the drinks. Perry adds two tablets of Rohypnol to each man's drink, clinks the glasses.

The older Greek guy is Yanni. He carries a little black leather handbag with him, that's what Perry wants to see. The younger guy is Kostas and he's happy and friendly. Katya likes him but Perry has told her the plan. They need more cash now he lied to her. The two men finish their drinks quickly. Yanni has his hands all over Perry, he reaches under her skirt as she sits on his knee in the big armchair. His hands reach along Perry's thighs, as he starts to get dizzy, he finds Perry's balls and is in shock for a few seconds, shaking his head, what the fuck is going on he thinks? He manages to push Perry off him who laughs out loud and Yanni staggers out of the chair. Kostas gets up from the other chair dizzy too, both men are fighting it, but the drug is too powerful. Katya has her hands over her eyes and Perry is still laughing as both men try to stand, try to fight it until there is nothing left to do except give up and lie down. Perry goes straight for the little black handbag.

There is a thousand in cash in the handbag and credit cards, she takes the cash, leaves the cards. Katya goes through Kostas' wallet and pants, finds another six hundred.

Perry says, 'Let's get out of here, we'll stay at The Hilton for a couple of nights, then Dylan will send through some more money.'

'Jesus, Perry, I told you. Don't tell Dylan about me. Don't even mention his name to me again, please. I can't stand it. If it's true. I can't stand it.'

'Grow up, baby, it's that awful Travis putting stupid thoughts in your head. It wasn't us. We didn't do anything. Dylan didn't do anything it was some crazy doing what crazies do.'

'Why the money then?'

'Oh, come on. I'm his sex slave whenever he wants me. He's coming to Melbourne; this money is an advance. Relax, babe, you'll like him.'

'Alright, alright, but if it's what...'

Perry kisses her on the cheek, hugs her, says, 'Let's get out of here, babe'

'If you say so.'

'I do. C'mon, we're going upmarket.'

CHAPTER EIGHTEEN

Travis drove fast along Old South Head Road. Ahn has told him she can't stay still, can't stay in her apartment in North Bondi. She has a key to his place and is waiting there for him. What the fuck was he going to say to her?

He scores a park out the front of his rented apartment on Lamrock Ave, walks up the steep stairs, down the side lane to the door. He unlocks the door but hears nothing as he closes it behind him. He walks into the kitchen. There is light coming through from the back door. It is open. Ahn is sitting there smoking. She had given up a couple of years ago.

Travis knelt down beside her, put his arm around her shoulder, saying, 'Sorry, mate. I mean, sorry, baby, I... it's pretty messed up. Billy playing around too much, once too often.'

'Nice and gentle, Travis, thanks. Only the facts, huh? No sympathy, and yeah I know you said sorry.'

'You knew him better than me. Look, those two guys are fucked up losers and somehow Billy fell in with them. They were high on E or something. Laughing and giggling even when the cops were there, it was bizarre.'

'That's Billy's life. Bizarre. From bad to great to me to this.'
'What can I do?'

She stands up, takes his hand, leads him back into the apartment, he pulls the back door closed with his free hand, she guides him through the kitchen to his bedroom. Sits on the bed, letting go of his hand, he says, 'Ahn, I don't...'

'Shhh,' she says putting her finger to her lips.

She takes off her cashmere sweater and bra, her breasts are small, round, perfect, her nipples a dark brown colour. She takes his hand again, makes him sit down. She kisses him, puts his hand on her right breast, he brushes her nipple with his thumb, kisses her back, tongues softly entwined. She puts her hand in his crotch, leaving it there, they keep kissing. He takes off his shirt. She pushes him back onto the bed. They both slip out of their jeans. She grabs his bum and pulls him to her. She stops kissing him for a few seconds saying, 'You can be a bit rough if you like.'

Permission granted.

Travis wakes up a bit dazed as ever. Takes in his surroundings, knows that he is home. Ahn isn't in bed. He can hear the TV in the lounge room but can't make out what she is watching. He gets up, puts on his jeans sans underwear, walks out of his room down the short hall and stops at the lounge entrance. She is sitting on the couch in her panties and one of his black T-shirts smoking and drinking coffee. Looks up at him, says, 'Thanks for last night.'

'It seems to be your answer to everything.'
'What! To fuck you? What the...'
'Not me. Oh yeah, look, forget it. I'm glad to be of assistance.'
'Thanks a lot for your sympathy at this time.'
'Ahn, you're here in my apartment. We fucked each other stupid last night. I think I can say I'm here for...'
'Right, right. Sorry.'

'What are you going to do?'

'I rang work. I can have three days off, then the funeral will come and go. I'll keep going straight ahead, moving, constantly moving forward if I can. I'll... I don't know. I'm going to have a shower, then take off.'

'Alright. You want some breakfast?'

She gets up from the couch, takes his hand again, this time leading him to the shower. She takes off the t-shirt, he strips off his jeans, hard already, she takes off her panties, grabs his cock as they get into the shower. She turns the hot water, adjusts it with the cold with one hand while stroking him with the other. They get under the water, he grabs her bum, lifts her up off the floor against the shower wall, water spraying, holds her there with his hands. She puts one arm around his neck, using her free hand to guide him inside her. Travis smiles and starts stroking in and out. Ahn holds him tight around the neck and starts grinding her hips back and forth against him.

———

They dress together in his bedroom, she in her jeans and a blue t-shirt she has borrowed from him, lastly slipping her black cashmere sweater over her head, adjusting it at the waist once it is on. Travis puts on black stretch Levi's, a black T, orange socks and black Docs. Searches for his brown suede jacket, finds it, puts it on, ready to roll.

'Ahn, I need my key back.'

'What?'

'My key, I need it back.'

'Why?'

'We're going to be working for two guys different guys who kiss in public but hate each other's guts in the real world.'

'You don't trust me?'

'Ahn, this is my shot back into the big time. Not playing footy, a different way in. He'll give me heaps of PI work. I know it.'

'Still love that sleazy world, don't you?'

'Not that shit again. I'll be working...'

'I know. You'll be working in his gambling clubs. Big step up.'

'Hey, what can I do? I can find people, you said it yourself. I found Billy. I can do good work for Andy Chiu. Work my way up. Fuck. I'm still young, Ahn.'

'Heard you had a girl with you at the game on Sunday.'

'And?'

'Getting all cocky again, feeling good, Travis.'

'The key, Ahn.'

She takes it from the money pocket of her jeans. A single key. Says, 'It's alright. I was giving you a hard time.'

'Can I give you a lift home?'

'Sure, where you going?'

'I'm going to see that girl, then I'm getting fitted for suits for...'

'I know what for.'

CHAPTER NINETEEN

Travis sits in the car outside of Ahn's place. Watches her walk up the stairs. She had been seriously in love with Billy. He knew that for certain, but she was one tough broad he thought, and smiled to himself at the word he used to describe her. Broad. Like a tough chick from a fifties noir film. But that was her. Hard as a cat's head.

He went through his phone, found Olsen's number and rang him leaving his number hidden.

'Olsen.'

'This is Travis Whyte.'

'Go on.'

'You find Perry?'

'Not my job, Mr Whyte. Your information has been passed on to the Melbourne boys. They'll find Perry if he's there.'

'Find, Perry, find the killer.'

'You keep fucken saying that. Why don't you find her or him? I hear you're good at finding people, albeit a little late with young Billy.'

'I found him though didn't I, and...'

'Now you're working for Andy Chui, you don't have time to find Perry, to find the guy who helped the killer set up that poor girl in that pissant little motel you worked in.'

'I... I might find time. It's not over, yet.'

'Piss off, loser, don't ring me again. I'm getting a case together against you.'

'Go for your life.'

Olsen ends the call. Travis feels guilty like he's never felt guilty before. He was right. Olsen was right.

He turns the ignition on in the old Dolomite Sprint, pushes a Peter Frampton tape in, does a U-turn headed for Potts Point to see Babus. To ask for a face to face with Farez. Something else he has no idea how to deal with. He'll wait until he is in the room with him to work it out.

Babus isn't home. Not answering her mobile. He gets out of the car. Calls Angelo who answers straight away and says, 'I heard about Billy. You did well to find him even if it was too late, you found him before the cops, before Ahn and...'

'Andy Chui said something about a tailor?'

Angelo coughed.

'Got you booked in tomorrow at a tailor in the Strand Arcade on George Street. He's my tailor too. Been in business since the dawn of time.'

'Good to know. What time?' He asks praying he says something afternoon-ish.'

'3 pm.'

'You're a good man, Angelo.'

'No second thoughts? This could lead to anything. Chui moves super-fast. If he likes you, the work you do, the sky, yeah, you know the cliché, but it's fucken true.'

Travis hadn't heard Angelo swear before. It had some kick to it.'

'I'm gonna do my best. But you should know. Olsen sent someone around to beat me up, only I got lucky. He reckons he's going to bring charges against me and...'

'He can't bring charges. And the other thing, did you say he sent someone around to...'

'Beat me up, yeah.'

'I'm going to let Chui know that. You know Olsen is under suspicion now. If Chui lets the right people know then it could be all over for him.'

'There's no proof. Only my word, and I don't know. I get the feeling that...'

Babus appears in front of Travis in long brown boots, a camel-coloured mini-skirt and black silk shirt, with two buttons undone, no bra.

He couldn't talk. She was amazing. Standing there, a shopping bag in each hand, smiling in front of his car.

'Hi,' he says.

'What?' Angelo says.

'I got girl problems, I'll ring you tomorrow,' he says and ends the call.

Angelo shrugs, girl problems? He rings Chui to tell him about Olsen sending someone to rough up Travis.

'Hi to you,' she says, puts the bags down.

Travis walks into her arms. She wraps them around his neck. He kisses her cheeks, she nuzzles into his neck, he kisses her eyes and mouth, she kisses him back, and then whispers in his ear, 'We better take this upstairs.'

Babus is wearing white satin panties and nothing else, standing a few feet back from the balcony, looking out at the view, the always grey but spectacular monolith of the Bridge slightly to the right, the white sails of the Opera House in front of it. It is raining hard, she's smoking. Travis is in the kitchen trying to work out the expensive coffee machine. He looks around the apartment while standing at the black granite benchtop. All-new, all the latest, ready to move into, the real estate slogan might go. Now is the time.

'I want to meet your brother, Farez.'

'I know.'

'Like yesterday.'

'Oh, you're the big hero who didn't make it in time.'

'You know about Billy.'

'It was on the news. The owner of Angel's nightclub found dead by private investigator, Travis Whyte, who was also working at the Cross Motel when Ann Gables was killed.'

'And?'

'You think Farez had something to do with it?'

'No. I don't think so. Those two, uh, they were high on something, fucked up in the head maybe before even getting high. Billy liked crazy people. He was one or had been until… and this is what bothers me. Ahn tells me how well he is doing. The manager at Angels says he is a genius at running the business, profits are high. But his girlfriend Ahn knows nothing about Farez who is supposed to at least part own it.'

Babus turns to face him, he can't take his eyes away from her flat stomach, her perfect round breasts, the white satin panties, she says, 'There's nothing unusual there. A silent partner; it happens everywhere.'

'But Farez's mobile number is on a mobile I find at Billy's place along with two other numbers. The manager and Shaun, who killed Billy. I ring Farez from Billy's mobile and say I'm Billy and he's upset, like, why the fuck are you ringing me upset. So, yeah, I want to meet him.'

'Stop staring at me.'

'Put some goddam clothes on. It's impossible to…'

She laughs out loud, walks quickly to the bedroom, closes the door.

He drinks his coffee on the balcony while smoking. If he looks to the left, he can see right into the apartments of people in a huge apartment building across the road. He thinks all kinds of kinky stuff might be going on behind all those closed curtains and some of the open ones, but nothing happens. It's the middle of the afternoon. Maybe the action starts later when the lights go down.

She appears from behind him, and Travis is slightly startled. She laughs again, says, 'A bit jittery, media star.'

'It's funny, I never watch the news. I didn't even know they'd put it all together like that. I had media training in Victoria when I was playing football.'

'Farez says he can see you tomorrow at his place in Coogee. 6 pm.

'You rang him.'

'Der. Don't be late. I'd get there early if I was you. He likes it when people are early because he's always on time, always.'

CHAPTER TWENTY

Travis goes home, does his research. The mood changed after she told him about the meeting. It was him not her. Farez owns clubs and strip joints on Darlinghurst Road, but he is a friend of the hugely popular right-wing radio personality Brian Smith. Smith is a little runt of a man who never talks but shouts everything as his little face turns red. A blowhard. And for some bizarre unknown reason, Sydney people have a love affair with their right-wing shock jocks. Melbourne would never have put up with his cheap vulgarity. But Farez is into real-estate too and dealing drugs because he is friends also with the leaders of two outlaw motorcycle gangs. His sister gets a mention on one website as a young socialite. Babus was beautiful, but Travis knew she was no socialite. She was tough and hard and had plenty of moves both in and out of bed but not a private-school girl.

Nothing happens to him or about him for the rest of the day. He hasn't sat still for an hour or more at one time since he got sacked from the Cross. A place where he had spent hours smoking, staring at the walls, or watching old movies on the ancient 'in-house' movie channel.

He does nothing, walks from room to room thinking. Then he

almost rings Babus to cancel the meeting with Farez. But doesn't. He can't see any connection between Andy Chui and Farez in research on the internet. That's good, but he wonders what he has to gain from meeting him now. Billy is dead at the hands of a couple of bent, gay, LSD trippers. He can't get Farez's voice out of his head though; what did he say, *since when do we meet,* or was it, *since when do you call me.* It wasn't friendly. There was some nastiness to it. He had given Billy's mobile to the cops. He wonders if they have spoken to Farez and the manager at Angels. Maybe Chui or Angelo could find out for him? He rang Angelo, but it went to voicemail. He didn't leave a message. He'd see him tomorrow.

He smokes a joint, gets into bed, feels relaxed. The front door is bolted. The windows locked. His gun is beside his bed. Olsen, he can't work out. Hell, Rogerson and Neddy Smith had been best mates. Anything could happen in this town. Chui might be able to protect him as well as advance his career. He has told him he knows where Travis lives. Where was the young Aboriginal boy? In his room with the million-dollar view, drunk? Stoned? But Travis has never seen the kid out of it. Even though he has that room, it's not secure. In essence, he lives on the streets, and that is more than enough to deal with. Perry and Katya. He still feels it. Feels he isn't doing the right thing. A girl died on his watch. The killer. Did he know where Travis lived?

CHAPTER TWENTY-ONE

Travis wakes up in the middle of the night. He can't breathe. He struggles to draw in a breath, gets up on his knees. Heart pumping. Struggles to stand trying to draw a breath. Tries to suck in air as he breaks through the fucken stupid portable clothes hanger trying to get to the window. He undoes the latch, pushes it open draws in huge breaths, heart still pumping, sweat running off his forehead. He pushes back past the clothes hanger. Lies down. Assumes the position, hand over his chest. Breathes in, breathes out, pushing his stomach out and one and two and three and four and five. Again. Breathing in and out, pushing his stomach out and one and two and three and four and five, and his breathing under control now.

Fuck.

They're coming more often these anxiety attacks. Or are they guilt attacks, he thinks. That girl died on my watch.

He wakes properly at 7 am. Puts his footy shorts on, an old white t-shirt, his Nike runners. Goes to the fridge, brings out cold water, drinks it fast and long, gets a bit of a cold freeze headache for a few seconds. Breaths out. He feels good. Unstoppable. Out the door, down the stairs to Lamrock Ave, running at a good clip towards the beach. There's this dog he sees all the time. Her tag has the name *Girl* scratched into it. She's like the dog from Footrot Flats. A Kelpie cross he thinks. Simply gorgeous and super friendly, he leans down, nuzzles his face into her head. She pushes back against his head. He scratches her belly. She rolls over onto her back. He says, 'Alright, Girl, you need a bit of tenderness.'

He scrunches her ears up, rubs the top of her head. She grins a great big stupid grin. He pats her head over and over smiling to himself. He's never met the owner.

'Gotta go, Girl.'

Off he runs across Campbell Parade, down the side street next to the Icebergs Club, down the stairs. He goes two at a time, the ocean crashing against the rocks metres away. The best early morning run in the world, he reckons, as he goes on past Mark's Park and Tamarama to Bronte. He feels like he could easy go onto Coogee and come back but turns around at Bronte, past the ocean swimming pool, along the front promenade. The ocean at his side, crashing waves, white water, surfers out at the best breaks, people come at him walking and jogging from the direction of Tamarama. He practically sprints the whole way back to the Icebergs he feels so good. Gotta stop smoking, he thinks, before it gets me. He reaches the corner of Lamrock Ave and Campbell Parade. A new café there. He stops in, buys a take-away, strong, flat white. Walks back the last few hundred metres to his apartment sipping the coffee thinking about the first cigarette of the day. He should eat something first or maybe make a coffee, sit down and light that first one of the day.

CHAPTER TWENTY-TWO

He walks into Albert's, the tailor shop, and Angelo is standing there at the desk with a beautiful girl with long, thick red hair. Travis does a double-take she is so pretty. Her blue eyes flash at him. He walks towards them both. Angelo says, 'Travis, this is my friend Dianne.'

Dianne puts out her hand, and Travis takes it as she says, 'What he meant to say was, this is my partner — as in girlfriend — Dianne.'

She gives Travis a firm handshake. Travis smiles, says, 'I can see the Sympatico between you.'

They both laugh, and Angelo says, 'You continue to surprise, Travis.'

'It's what I do.'

'Dianne is leaving now, I think.'

And she smiles at him, says, 'Yeah, have to rush, nice to meet you, Travis.'

'Same,' he says.

And as Dianne leaves, Angelo says, 'He'll be out in a sec. He's old but brilliant. Be patient.'

'I'm starting to think I let that girl down badly. I'm not starting to think. I know I let her down.'

'I don't know what you think you're going to do, Travis. Let the police do it.'

'I can find people.'

'So can the police. You're at a turning point in your life.'

An old guy with grey hair, grey pants, impossibly shiny black shoes, a white shirt, and blue cardigan comes out of a backroom, a tape measure around his neck, saying, 'Hello, hello, you must be Travis. We have work to do here, Angelo.'

'It's all paid for, Travis. See you tomorrow night at the Club.'

'See you, Angelo.'

At around four in the afternoon, Travis walks out. The suits will be ready tomorrow midday. He has a couple of hours to kill. Babus said get there early. He will.

He sits in a café where the old Gowings store used to be. He used to like shopping there. It was inexpensive, the staff never pushy. There didn't seem to be any order to the place. Shit was everywhere. You wouldn't buy a suit there. But shirts, shorts, and t-shirts were cool. They had a barber where you could get a $10 haircut, and that was only three or four years ago.

He sips the coffee slowly, tapping his hand on the tabletop. He stops. Picks up his mobile, calls Katya. She answers.

'Where are you?'

'Leave me alone, Travis.'

'What?'

'I mean, I don't know what I mean. Give me space.'

She hangs up.

He calls the legendary Bodie.

'Hello.'

'Bodie, it's Travis.'

'Nice to hear your voice, friend.'

'Do you know where Katya is?'

'I heard all about what happened.'

'That's not what I asked you.'
'What's got into you brother. I'm your friend.'
'I'm sorry. It's important.'
'Alright, but no, no I don't know. Can we catch up sometime?'
'Yeah, I'd like that. Early next week, once the game is out of the way on Sunday?'
'Alright, call, let me know where.'
'Thanks, Bodie.'

He finishes his coffee. Walks the short distance to behind the magnificence of the late nineteenth century Queen Victoria Building where he parked his car. Pierre Cardin once said it was the most beautiful shopping centre in the world. He gets in and starts her up. He will be in Coogee about 5.30 given it is practically peak hour. He hopes Farez likes him. He hopes shit doesn't get out of hand because he likes Babus. A lot. Maybe too much too soon.

CHAPTER TWENTY-THREE

Farez lives on Dolphin Street about a five-minute walk to the beach in a two-storey black and white concrete apartment. Impregnable is the impression. A black security gate for the car and pedestrian access. Travis pushes the intercom, waits. A few seconds go by then ten seconds, twenty seconds. Travis reaches to push it again, but a voice says, 'Travis Whyte?'

'Yes.'

'Push the gate now.' A buzzing noise goes off, and Travis pushes the gate open, walks up the white stairs to the black front door. As he reaches it, the door is pulled open, and a big guy, like a bodybuilder type but short in stature, opens the door.

Travis says, 'Farez?'

'No, I'm Dima. Come in, follow me,' the big guys says and leads him down a hallway to an open door. Travis looks into the room, Dima says, 'Wait in there. Farez won't be long. Help yourself to a drink,' and walks off.

He's in a small theatrette with a big screen that takes up most of the back wall. There is a small bar to the left with enough room for three barstools, each with leopard print cushions on them. There are a couple of large two-seater black sofas side by side. Spare chairs higgledy-piggledy around the place. Travis walks behind the small bar, opens the fridge. He finds a bottle of lemonade and a glass. There is a small ice machine. He takes enough for his drink from the open tray at the bottom. There is an ashtray on the bar. He lights a cigarette, puts his arse on one of the leopard print cushions, draws in deeply, blows the smoke high into the air, takes a sip of his drink. He has plenty of cash at the moment. More than he needs, and tonight and tomorrow will bring more cash, but he hasn't had time to get high and go out or have a day betting on the horses, and the compulsion to gamble has mysteriously left him for the moment. He likes it. He has money; why gamble?

The door opens. A tall thin man in black chinos and a white linen shirt enters the room. He puts out his hand, says, 'Travis, I'm Farez.'

Farez goes behind the bar, looks at Travis. Travis looks back hard. Farez has some deep acne scars on his right cheek and small little scars like big shaving nicks across his forehead. Maybe he was glassed, Travis thinks, back in the past when he was on his way up. Farez smiles. Travis sees straighter than straight and whiter than white teeth. All achieved with the help of an expensive dentist. The rough hew of his face mixed with the perfect teeth gives him a compelling look. Cool but dangerous. He has curly black hair cut short. He says to Travis, 'Another drink?'

'No, er, maybe you can top it up. It's lemonade.'

Farez tops up the lemonade. Pours himself a dry ginger ale, says to Travis while lifting his glass, 'To sobriety.'

Travis laughs, drinks, says, 'I do like a drink but not now.'

'Me too,' Farez says and laughs.

There is silence for a whole minute, maybe longer. Finally, Farez says, 'What do you want?'

'You know I found Billy.'

'Too late though, Travis.'

'Yeah, that's right. I found a mobile phone at Billy's place in Darlinghurst. It had three numbers in it.'

Travis stops talking for ten seconds, takes another sip on his lemonade.

'It had three names in the contacts list. You, the manager of Angels, and Shaun who helped kill him. I rang you from that mobile and said I was Billy, and you weren't happy. Why?'

'None of your business.'

'Do you have part ownership of Angels?'

'I have the full ownership of Angels. Billy was the manager; he did a great job once he started taking my advice.'

'But his girlfriend tells me that...'

'Billy was keen to impress Ahn and her father. To show that he had changed. I paid him a lot of money. He was doing well.'

'But when I rang you saying I was Billy...'

'Once again. None of your business. I will come to a financial arrangement with Ahn in due course.'

Travis is shot down. He's got nothing.

'You and my sister are seeing each other?'

'Yes.'

'Look after her, Travis. I have to go. Dima will see you out,' he says walking from behind the bar to towards the door.

'One more thing,' Travis says, 'have the police spoken to you?'

Farez leaves the room without replying.

CHAPTER TWENTY-FOUR

Katya and Perry spent a few nights at the Hilton in East Melbourne. They kept low key after checking in, watched movies, ordered room service, never opening the door, asking for the trays to be left outside. The room wasn't serviced, they left the towels outside the door, and the housemaids brought clean ones and toilet paper. They didn't touch the mini-bar; they had supplies of their own. Perry was nervous about Katya.

They checked into another Airbnb on the morning Travis was due to start at Andy Chui's gambling club. They never met the host, because there was a code to the front door and to the apartment in Preston. It was a two-bedroom job, plain and ordinary in a plain and ordinary block of cream-brick apartments in a back street behind the High Street shopping Centre. Perry has many ID's. It doesn't matter. He is Dom Martin for this place. Perry doesn't think Travis will come looking, but if he does, he won't be looking in Preston. He will think Perry is in St Kilda or around Chapel Street, maybe Richmond or South Yarra, places full of colour and verve, cafés, bars, and all-night entertainment. Preston has some of this, Northcote and Thornbury close by has more. She and Katya can still do all these things, go out, get crazy, but come back to Preston to sleep and relax. Perry knows that Travis thinks she is evil; a 'waster' he once called him.

Perry thinks Travis loves Katya, maybe is *in love* with her. But Katya loves Perry like a daughter loves her mother. Dylan is coming tomorrow, and Perry is thrilled about it. Dylan is clever, full of ideas, devious like himself, and he has money. Perry doesn't know where it comes from, but she wants it, as much as she can get of it. Did he kill the girl at the Cross Motel? Perry doesn't know, but who else could it be? The description that Travis gave the police that they then put in the paper, it was Dylan, but it was also several thousand other thirty-year-old guys. He isn't great looking, Mr Dylan, but he is dangerous, and Perry likes that more than anything.

CHAPTER TWENTY-FIVE

TRAVIS IS INTRODUCED AROUND TO EVERYONE AT THE DEN. This is the name of the gambling club that lives in a quiet side street off Macleay Street in Potts Point, a few hundred metres from the dirty-half-mile of Kings Cross. There are no signs anywhere with the name of the club on it. It is the bottom floor of a mid-sized Victorian mansion. There were bedrooms upstairs with girls waiting in a kind of elegant common room with a female supervisor by the name of Cherry, waiting for the winners to celebrate, the losers to whinge, fuck, and go home.

Travis knows what he has to do. There is a password that changes every night. If the guests don't know the password, they don't get in. Travis is working with a guy called Wicky. Older guy with a DK Lillee moustache, tall and broad-shouldered, he seems to come from a different time. His hair is cut short with loose tails at the back. He says to Travis as three people come up the drive to the front door, 'Even if they've been here twenty times before, it doesn't matter. If they didn't get the new password, there's a reason. We don't need to know the reason; we do what they pay us to do. Flash that gun holster of yours and most pricks back off. The women are the fucken worst.

How dare you and so on? If it gets tricky, we get Cherry from upstairs to help talk some sense into them. Try not to lay a hand on any women at all, ever. Now, let's see if these cunts have the password.'

One of the men from the group of three grabs the ornate knocker, bangs it into the door three times, loud. Wicky rolls his eyes, opens the door, 'Password, gents.'

The guy looks at him, says, 'Vodka martini and be quick about it.'

'Don't fuck with me, sir,' Wicky says, 'password or piss off.'

Travis smiles broadly at his new friend, the male guest coughs a few times, says, 'Ginger.'

'Welcome to The Den, sir, and good luck.'

Travis gets tipped a hundred dollar note a few times for letting people in. A few other guys put $50 notes in his hand, twenties also. Good, clean, old-fashioned cash in hand, no tax money. The job is a doddle, he thinks, but Wicky keeps saying to him, 'Don't relax. When you relax, shit happens, and Mr Chui does not like shit to happen.'

Wicky lets him 'have a wander' after a few hours when there is a lull. He walks all through the club. The women are mostly thin and blond, all teeth and lips that look like they been injected with some strange fluid. A brunette stands out with a silver backless dress. A young Asian girl he thinks might be Chinese is beautiful in a black jumpsuit. The guys are mostly loud and obnoxious, and then there's a few professional punters, cool, calm quiet types, trying to beat the bank, but the bank never loses; not the type of money that could change your life. The place is decked out with brown and black leather sofas against the walls. A bar in the corner of the main gambling room is surprisingly small. You can't sit there and have a drink; there's no room. Chui wants his guests at the gambling tables. A couple of girls in black pencil skirts, white shirts, three buttons undone, and black bras visible, plus one other guy in black and whites and a bow tie ferrying drinks from the bar to the tables. The night goes on uneventful.

Travis gets home around 8 am, throws the tip money on the table, gets a drink of cold water from the fridge, sits and counts out the notes. $700 in tips for one night, but he hated the dickwads who handed it out like he was some kind of a necessary afterthought. He gets up, strips off his suit in the bathroom, gets in the shower, stays in there for twenty minutes thinking about the night. Then he starts thinking about Babus and gets out, walks naked from the shower to his bedroom, closes the curtains on the small window, and gets into bed.

He wakes up at 5 pm. He has to start work at 10 pm. That $700 is aching to be spent. He showers again, dresses in old blue Levi's 501's, a black t-shirt, pulls a black polo neck knit on over his head. Puts his socks and Doc Martin's on. Gets his second suit and clean white shirt and tie, puts them on a hanger, goes out to the car. Hangs the suit up in the back on a clip by the top of the back window. Drives to the car park on Ward Ave that he used to park in when he worked at The Cross Motel. The code is still the same. He parks, walks around to the Crest Hotel, goes up to the bar on the first floor. They have the races live on a big screen. He orders a beer and a Bourbon shot. His evening begins alone, even though he's sure to know people in the Goldfish Bowl bar down on the street level. Gambling is a solo trip for Travis.

He bets and drinks and bets and drinks. After a couple of hours, the barman is sick of the sight of him because he is betting crazy on nearly every race across horses, harness, and greyhounds. The barman had planned an easy night. No-one came to this dive anymore. The whole hotel was up for sale. They keep this bar open for guests, but no-one ever comes. An hour ago, the barman paid out a grand to Travis, but old Travis, he put five-hundred on the nose on a twenty-to-one shot. Plus a few other bets of a hundred dollars each and another beer with a Bourbon chaser and he bets and drinks and bets and it is ten o'clock. He can't face the whole set-up again. It was too fancy. Too awful, accepting those hundred-dollar tips from fuckers he wouldn't piss on. At the Cross Motel, it was check-in blah blah have a good time, but Travis liked it. He liked telling people all the cool spots to go to. How to get where. He sympathised with the lonely old men coming in the middle of the night or during the day to call up a hooker or pick one off the street. They were sad, yeah, but he liked them. He liked standing on the front stoop of the Motel, watching the crazy street light up and close down. Especially, he liked it when it was raining on a busy Friday night or an oh-so-lonely, so-sad, Tuesday night at 11 pm. People walking heads bowed, the spruikers huddled around the entrance to the clubs, not spruiking, laughing, and telling jokes, cos no-one was around. The die-hard girls on the street still, oh-so-sad and lonely and beautiful. Paul Kelly wrote a beautiful line in a song about it.

Travis stands up, thanks the barman. He's a bit pissed alright, worn-out too. In the lift down he counts his cash. $285 and change. Enough for a big night. He walks along Darlinghurst Road through the body-to-body crowd of an early night-time Kings Cross. Makes his way to the Cross Motel. The door is unlocked. Gavin is handing some old guy with a bald patch at the back of his head a key to a room. He smiles when he sees Travis. The old bloke gets in the lift. Travis says, 'Gavin, my man, still doing the twelve-hour shifts?'

'You're a bit pissed, mate.'

'I am.'

"I thought, I, um, heard you were working in some club or…'

'No more, no more. I need some speed, mate. I'm getting tired, and I got a whole night ahead of me.'

'Come in the back.'

Travis snorts two lines, and drunk, laughs to himself, says to Gavin, 'Thanks, man. How much do I owe you?'

'One-twenty for the two grams. The lines are on the house.'

'Kind of you, Gav. I need to make a call or two.'

'Go ahead.'

Travis calls Bodie at the sex shop on Oxford Street, Darlinghurst. He answers, and Travis recognises his voice.

'Boooodie, what time do you finish work, man?'

'Eleven.'

'Let's go out drinking and see some music. Gonna get high as a kite like that.'

'Sounds like you already started, but yeah. I can get a taxi wherever you want.'

'You know the Cross Motel where I used to work?'

'Yeah.'

'See you in an hour, Booooodie.'

'I'll see you, Trav. Take it easy, man.'

Travis calls up Ahn.

'Hello.'

'Ahn baby.'

'Oh, baby, baby, baby. You must be drunk.'

'I am.'

'What happened, Travis, that club not sleazy enough for you? Did you at least ring Andy Chui?'

'Nope. Nice clean break.'

'Messy, more like it. You know he's going to come looking for you at some stage.'

'Come to the Cross Motel. Booooodie will be here in an hour.'

'Bodie, oh my God. You are drunk. The sex shop stud.'

'The one and only. Come, come, please say you'll come.'

'I will. You going to tell me about this Farez character?'

Travis sobers up for a second or three, rubs his forehead hard with the heel of his hand, says, 'Has he called you?'

'No.'

'Ok, Ok, Ok, um, see you soon. You can meet Babus if I can reach her.'

'Great. I'll be there in an hour.'

Travis calls Babus. She answers, and he's ecstatic, says, 'I am sooo glad you picked up. Have you made any plans?'

'It's Friday night. I'm making plans now.'

'What are they?'

'I'm going to the Kardomah.'

'Ah, where we met. Is it alright if me, Ahn, and Bodie come along?'

'Yes, I want to see you.'

'I have some speed.'

'You want to come to my apartment first? We won't be leaving until midnight at least.'

'Yes, yes, yes. I'll see you in an hour, cool?'

'What happened?'

'I can't be controlled.'

'Ha Ha Ha. No job can hold you. Not even for two nights.'

'I have a job. I'm a PI.'

'Farez said to me, no wait, I'll tell you when you get here.'

'See you soon.'

He hangs up, says to Gavin, 'Ok, if I hang out in the back office here for an hour until Ahn gets here? You know Ahn?'

'Yeah, I know Ahn. She's beautiful, and you're always welcome, mate. Straight or bent or whatever, dude.'

'Thanks, man.'

CHAPTER TWENTY-SIX

Bodie, all 195cm of him, walks into the reception area. Travis is on the brown, cheap, cracked vinyl couch in the foyer, checking Instagram. He looks up, smiles, says, 'Bodie, good to see you.'

He gets up, and they man hug for a few seconds. Travis steps back from him. Bodie has black shoulder-length hair, brown eyes like chocolate drops, is broad-shouldered, wearing black jeans, a long-sleeved green t-shirt under a grey t-shirt that says Youth Revolution. Bodie is thirty years old. He hasn't shaved for a day or two. He has cheekbones models would die for. Travis says, 'How's the sex trade?'

'Oh, you know, kinkies, pedos, straights, gays, er trans, any known, um, LGTBI, and glory holes all that kind of shit.'

Travis laughs out loud as does Gavin who heard what he said and is now standing at reception.

'You must be Bodie,' he says.

Bodie says, 'That's me. I hear you got some good speed?'

Gavin smiles, says, 'Let's adjourn to the back office.'

'Adjourning,' says Travis.

A few guests come and go while Travis and Bodie are out the

back snorting lines. Gavin deals with them as best as he can as always. He has an amazing attitude to this work. He finds that if he does the best job he can possibly do, he enjoys it more. It spurs him on a bit, like how Travis likes the odd bods, the weirdos, but he also likes the families who aren't sure what to expect of this inexpensive motel in the heart of sin city. He is their spirit guide advising them of journeys and travels from Bondi to Newtown to Glebe and on the ferry to Manly, and you should walk along to Victoria Street to all the cafés, and don't be worried about safety; walk with purpose wherever you're walking to and from.

Things have changed since Ann was brought here and butchered. Cancellations all over the place, but still a steady stream. He has extra work now that Travis is gone.

Bodie stands up.

'Where can I take a piss,' he says, and Gavin shows him the way out to the courtyard. Ahn arrives knocking on the door after Gavin locked it at 11 pm. He gets up, and when he sees it is Ahn he rushes a bit faster, unlocks it, pulls the door back.

Ahn says, 'Gavin, hi, long time.'

She is wearing a black Julie Newmar-style catsuit.

Gavin hugs her, which Ahn isn't expecting. She has her arms straight by her side, and she kind of spins and almost teeters after Gavin lets her go. She smiles at him, and he says, 'Yeah, it's good to see you. You look amazing.'

Gavin stares at her for too long before realising, turns away, yells, 'It's Ahn.'

Travis has his head over another line and snorts it right up. Ahn is shown out to the back office. Travis grabs her and kisses her on the mouth, she pulls away saying, 'Bloody hell, Travis.'

'You look amazing.'

'Thanks. Keep those hands to yourself tonight if the famous Babus is coming.'

Travis looks suitably chastised. Ahn says, 'Ring Andy Chui. Tell him something.'

"No, no. It's too late now.'

"It's never too late, Travis.'

'Ok, ok, when we get to Babus' place. This is where it happened, Ahn. Where I let that girl down.'

'Please, Travis, not now. We're all going out to have a good time. And you know I have my own sorrows.'

Bodie walks back in. Ahn smiles and looks up at him, 'Nice to see you, Bodie man. You look enormous as always.'

Everyone laughs and Travis says, 'Gee, Gav, I wish you could come with us.'

'Yeah, no can do, but have a great night. Good to meet you, Bodie.'

'Yeah, same here Gavin. I know where to come if I need anything.'

'For sure. Only give me a call first, unlike Travis.'

'Let's go,' Travis says, 'into the night.'

The three of them walk along behind the reception desk, then out through the foyer. Travis unlocks the door, opens it wide, yells out, 'Thanks, Gav, hope it's a quiet night.'

They launch out onto Darlinghurst Road, Ahn in the middle, Travis and Bodie on either side of her, stepping around and almost through people. Zigging and zagging until they are seventy metres down Macleay Street where the crowd has thinned out and they can mostly walk three across the footpath, chat and talk and laugh. They reach her building, and Travis says to both of them, 'You are going to love Babus.'

They go up in the lift and reach the front door.

Thousands of different scenarios ready to be played out all over the big wide city.

CHAPTER TWENTY-SEVEN

Babus opens the door, and Travis reaches for her. She lets him grab her, and he picks her up underneath her arms, twirls her around. She screams with laughter. Bodie laughs, and Ahn looks on a bit shocked. Is Travis in love, she wonders, so soon? He puts her down and introduces Bodie and Ahn. She kisses them both once on each cheek, and they all walk into the big lounge area.

Four girls are sitting around the room each with a drink in her hand. One striking looking black girl. A girl who looks about thirty and has braces on her teeth. Two slim brown-haired girls who are that alike they must be sisters. Babus introduces everyone around, and Bodie makes straight for the two brown haired sisters. Ahn sits next to Babus on a sofa. Travis stands in the middle of the room. Babus says, 'Farez is coming with about twelve people. He had some alcohol delivered. It's all behind the bar, Travis. Help yourself. Get drinks for your friends.'

'I don't mind being the barman,' Travis says. 'Bodie? Ahn?'
'Beer for me, any kind,' Bodie says.
'Is there Vodka?' Ahn asks.
'Everything,' Babus says. 'My brother sent over everything.'

'Then a Vodka with coke,' she says.
'With coke?' Travis asks.
'Yeah, Coke. It's my new thing.'

Travis makes the drinks thinking all the time about Farez coming over with 'about twelve people'. He isn't in the best shape to impress anyone. He is feeling exhausted, even with the speed. He delivers the drinks and then grabs Babus by the hand and leads her to her bedroom.

She says, 'Travis, I have guests, we can't...'
'I know. I know. I have some speed. You want some?'
'Yeah, I do, but if my brother ever asks you, I never go near chemical drugs. I mean speed or coke or smack or LSD or acid or whatever, ice, whatever the latest thing is. I never touch it; only grass and alcohol. Nothing else. If he knows you give me...'
'I get the idea. You don't have to educate me. I mean. No, no, it's a good thing you told me. Shall I cut the lines on the sink or...'
'I have a book. A little black book.'

She goes to a small bookshelf. It is a Catholic Bible.
'Normally they're not black, are they?' he asks.
'This one is.'
'Alright.'

He cuts up three lines.
'Two for you, one for me cos I already had some and... yeah. I already had some.'

Babus takes a fifty from Travis and rolls it up, snorts one line, then the second, says, 'I have to get back to my girls.'
'Alright, alright.'

Travis lies down on the bed and the bible falls onto the floor, but he can't be bothered picking it up. He lifts himself right up onto the bed. Drags himself up to the head of the bed and pulls back the black doona and puts his head on the pillow and can hear himself breathe. Ten days ago, Ann died. He found those the two shitheads that killed Billy. He met Babus. He got the Aboriginal kid a game. He played for Randwick as usual. He let down Andy Chui, one of the biggest players in Sydney. He wonders what Wicky is thinking. They would have dragged some guy in to do his job. Why didn't he ring Andy Chui? As if he doesn't have enough enemies already. Now Olsen and Chui both will be... and he closes his eyes and kicks his shoes off. If anyone ever should be truly exhausted, it is Travis.

Ten minutes later, Babus walks back into her bedroom and sees him asleep on the bed. She knows what he has done these past two weeks. She gets a rug from the walk-in wardrobe and gently puts it over him. He's a handsome man, she thinks, full of life. She was super impressed when she saw him play for Randwick. He carried the team that day, even she who knew nothing about the game could see that. She gets a dustpan and brush from the kitchen as Farez rings the doorbell, his entourage all standing behind him. She cleans up the speed and empties the contents into the bin and puts the Bible back on the shelf.

Bodie tries to open the front door, but it is locked. Babus comes rushing out of the bedroom and quickly unlocks the front door, and Farez is standing there, and she grabs him by the hand and says, 'Come in, come in.'

He hugs her, she kisses him on the corner of the lips and the others file in, and Farez says, 'Too many people for introductions. Everybody relax, find someone you like, talk to them, be happy. All of the drinks are behind the bar. Dima, can you run the bar for an hour to get everything started.'

Dima walks behind the bar, and the new arrivals move there, and Farez says to Babus, 'Where is he? Where is Travis?'

CHAPTER TWENTY-EIGHT

TRAVIS WAKES UP THE NEXT MORNING NOT SURE WHERE HE IS. He takes a while, lies still but opens his eyes slightly. Slowly he gets accustomed to the dim light. He's sleeping on a bed, a rug over him. Looks to his left. Babus is asleep under the covers. The doona pulled right up to her chin. He takes the rug off and sits up. What the fuck time is it? I got to play today, he thinks. He sees his mobile on the floor at his feet. Picks it up. 10 am. Alright, the game is at midday today. He has time to drive home, get changed, have something to eat.

He stands up. Decides to let Babus sleep. What happened last night, he wonders. That speed barely affected him. Ten days of shit hitting the fan knocked me out, he thinks. It is a lot of shit too. Now, he has to deal with Andy Chui. He'll call him after the game. He doesn't want to alter his mood with a negative call.

He wanders into the lounge room. Sees Ahn asleep on one of the big sofas, looks around for Bodie, nowhere to be seen. No-one else there, not in the lounge anyway. He walks back down the hall to the second bedroom, knocks on the door and enters slowly. Bed empty. Bodie got himself home. He gently puts his hand on Ahn's shoulder. She is fully clothed, a rug trapped under her waist. She doesn't move.

He gently rocks her, and her eyes open, and she blinks a few times, and Travis smiles, remembers falling in love with her. She's amazing in her catsuit, with her shaved head, dark eyebrows, beautiful black eyes. He bends down and kisses her on the cheek.

'Hey,' she goes, 'how are you? I was worried about you crashing out like that. It's not...'

'Not normal. Not for me.'

'Yeah.'

'I feel great, but I'm playing today. You want a lift home now, maybe hit Maccas in The Cross first? You hungry, baby?'

'Now I'm your baby again?'

'C'mon. Two Cheeseburgers, large fries each, a big chocolate thick shake each, an apple pie or two. No more hangover.'

'Alright. It sounds pretty good. I'm tired of being sad, Travis. I miss Billy a lot. Farez said he'd call me on Monday. Organise a meeting. Explain everything.'

'Can I suggest you take Angelo with you and that you ring your old man and your boss first? See if they have any knowledge of this guy that you can use as leverage in the discussions about the nightclub, make sure he's not ripping you off, go through Billy's papers at your place, and I mean do it properly. Try and find some sort of certificate of ownership. Ask that manager who loves Billy about it. Try and get into the safe at the nightclub, and I mean ask Angelo to get someone to fucken break-in. I mean it.'

'Whoa, could you write down this stuff for me?'

'I'll send you and Angelo an email when I get home. I should have told him all this, but I had to wait and see what Farez would do. I can't stand typing long messages into my mobile, so wait for the email. Now, let's eat.'

'Oh, yeah, Travis. A chocolate thick shake with a freeze headache coming up.'

They both laugh.

Ahn gets up. Travis finds the front door keys in a brightly coloured bowl on the big, flat, wooden coffee table. Shakes them in his hands. They walk to the door; he opens it with the keys. It will lock when he pulls it to from the outside. He throws the keys aiming for the bowl, misses, and they smash into a glass that gets knocked to the floor. They both giggle at each other and leave.

Ahn got a few salacious looks in her catsuit at Maccas. Travis bought a third cheeseburger to take with him for the drive. They drive along New South Head Road past Rushcutters Bay. The marina is visible and full of boats on their left as they drive up past the park and now through Edgecliff. Travis turns right onto Ocean Street and remembers the young Aboriginal boy and calls him while steering with one hand.

'Hello,' the boy answers.

'Paul. Its Travis.'

'Hi.'

'Did you train? Did you get a game yesterday? Did they pick you?'

'Ha Ha Ha. All the questions, footballer.'

'Well, did you?'

'Training was good. I like the people there. No shit. No, do this, do that. I got a game, started on interchange.'

'And?'

'I kicked a few goals, then they gave me a run in the midfield. Did alright. But not fit enough yet.'

'Kicked a few goals! Are you shitting me?'

'No, brother. Kicked a few goals. One from a sharp angle. Impress that coach ha ha ha.'

'Can you come to the seniors game today? Do you need a lift?'

'Yeah, yeah, that would be good. I'm still at the same place. Ring me when you downstairs.'

The boy hangs up.

Something positive, Travis thinks. At last.

———

He drops off Ahn. He opens the door to his apartment with a little rise in heartbeat and blood temperature. Andy Chui saying, *I know where you live.* Olsen sending round bent cops to bash him. Nothing. Nada. No surprises. He showers and changes into jeans and a loose black t-shirt that has *Los Angeles* written on it in blue. Puts on black desert boots. Packs his footy gear into a blue Adidas bag. Gets his laptop out and sends the emails to Ahn and Angelo, breathes out and breathes in and out a few more times. Football today. On the ground being the only place he is in total control.

He calls Paul from outside the squat in Darlinghurst. He comes out the rusted front gate, a smile on his face. It makes Travis smile too. Maybe this kid can do bigger things, he thinks. He's what, sixteen, but he has to see him play first. He's getting carried away.

Paul hops in the front seat, and Travis put out his hand. 'Three goals on debut; you're doing all right. Do you have boots and training gear and...?'

'Boss at the club fixed me up with boots and gear,' he says, and Travis sees in the moment, hears in his voice, some emotion, like his voice is going to crack, but he doesn't. He smiles, says, 'Thanks, footballer. Looking forward to seeing you play, learn a few tricks from the gubba.'

Travis takes off fast and puts a tape in the ancient tape deck. Bob Seger starts singing Hollywood Nights and he turns it up. His old man used to play it loud at night when he came home, when his mum still lived with them. He had mixed memories about it but loved the song. He must ring his father.

Travis plays the first couple of quarters in the midfield, but Randwick is down by three goals at half-time. The coach shifts Travis forward, deep forward, so someone has to take him one on one, which is a win for Randwick. No-one can go with him. The coach replaces him in the midfield with a young guy off the half-back-flank. It is the making of the young player. He wins plenty of contested balls and sends it in deep to Travis who kicks five goals in the second half, and Randwick win again. Paul watches on, taking mental notes. One day he might play in the seniors, but for now, he is happy.

Travis drops Paul off at home and does a U-turn, heads up to Oxford Street, turns left for Bondi. He drives quickly thinking about his conversation with Ahn that morning. Had he been talking loudly? Had Ahn been loud? He hoped to God that Babus hadn't heard him talking about tactics for dealing with Farez. He makes it home and walks in the door and immediately his mobile phone goes off. He sees the caller ID. It is Ahn, he answers, 'What's up. I...'

'Hello, baby.'

'Hi, you sound, um, a...'

'A little frustrated, yeah, baby. I liked it when you called me that this morning. Can you come over?'

'I'll be there in half-an-hour.'

CHAPTER TWENTY-NINE

Travis gets home at 8 am. Ahn rushed off to work, and he had to leave. He made a brief supermarket stop on the way home. He gets a white bowl from the cupboard. He throws in a dozen raspberries. He likes the red on the white bowl. I'm crazy, he thinks. Opens the Greek yogurt and dishes six tablespoons of the thickest Greek yogurt into the bowl, opens up the Weet-Bix and crushes two into the yogurt and raspberries. Turns on the news and catches the sport round-up, which is what he hoped for. He thinks of babus and what an arsehole he is. But maybe she's already done to him. He doubts it. They have rare chemistry. He cannot say no to Ahn, knows he will have to, but she is so deliciously bad in bed.

There's a knock on the door. Fuck is this, he thinks at 8.30. He gets up and opens the front door. Andy Chui is standing there in a black suit, white shirt, thin black tie. The suit looks expensive, and Travis says, 'Good morning,' and then he can't breathe. Another attack. He puts up his hand and Chui watches him in disbelief as he kneels down and tries to catch his breath.

Chui says, 'Travis, are you alright? What the hell. Open the door. Open the door.'

Travis stands up and gulps in air searching for a breath. He can't get it, squats down again, puts his hand over his chest and slowly, slowly, he gets some air into his lungs. Chui looks at him like he's crazy. He has his palm flat on the wire screen door now as he stands up.

'Not again, fuck, not again,' he says, and then he can breathe a little better, and he opens the door, motions Andy Chui in, and he still has his palm up, meaning, wait, wait. And Chui waits and Travis gets nearly back to normal and says, 'Get these attacks every now and then. Anxiety. Probably best I don't work for you anymore.'

Chui stands up straight, looks him in the eye and says, 'You owe me.'

'I can't do that sort of work. Shitheads looking at me like I'm nothing while they put a $100 in the top pocket of that suit you bought me.'

'Suits.'

'Oh, yeah, suits.'

'You can keep them. They're bespoke, they won't fit anyone else.'

'Appreciate it, but I doubt if I'll ever wear them again.'

'I want you to go to Melbourne for me.'

'What?'

'Two Vietnamese guys stole three hundred K from me. It was drug money.'

'And?'

'They're Melbourne guys. I don't have any sway in Melbourne. Sydney is my place. You know Melbourne.'

'I used to know Melbourne.'

'You know Melbourne; the Melbourne that deals with drugs and crims and...'

'Hey, hey, I...'

'I know what happened. What cancelled your ticket to the big time. I know about your father. What he did. What he was like before he quit drinking and drugs.'

Travis doesn't reply. This is his chance, and Chui is going to pay him for it.

'Travis?'

'I'll do it. You got any other information on these guys?'

'Angelo will email you photos and their names, all we know about them. Past dealings. You have to leave today. Fly, not drive. I'll have a hire car for you at Tullamarine. The Hertz desk.'

'What's my cut?'

'Twenty K.'

'Hmmm.'

'You think 300 K is a lot of money? It's not. It's nothing. You couldn't buy a tiny apartment in Bondi with it, not even a grubby little studio apartment. Nothing. Can't change your life, not enough for that. My tip is they'll try and buy drugs. Most likely ice, to deal, then it can change their life. They can make ten times that 300k. More if they're smart. I know you have Vietnamese friends through Ahn and her father, and you know people in the drug trade.'

'You going to book a flight or…'

'You're on the 2.30 to Melbourne. Tiger Airways. Seat 1A.'

'Beautiful.'

'Angelo has probably already sent that email to you. He'll send you the boarding pass. When you have done what I ask and you want to come back, email Angelo again. He'll book a flight. But you must find that money. I can't have these people stealing from me. It's bad for business and my reputation.'

'I'm sorry I let you down, I…'

'You don't care much about anyone, but it might come in handy searching for these men. You're not scared of anything, but you better get some help for those panic attacks. In your game, it could cost you your life.'

I get scared, Travis thinks, only I don't show it.

'I better pack, I guess.'

'Don't let me down, Travis.'

'No.'

Chui hands him an envelope, says, 'Your travel expenses. Not part of the twenty K by the way.'

'Thanks.'

'I'm leaving.'

'Right.'

Chui turns and walks back out the door, and Travis follows him and locks the wire door after him, closes the front door, locks it.

He's going to find Katya and Perry. And it was handed to him.

He rings Olsen.

'Hello.'

'I'm going to Melbourne. Going to find the crossdresser and the hooker.'

'Not before time. But I can't help you.'

Olsen hangs up.

Travis calls Ahn.

'I'm going to Melbourne later today. I've been hired to find some people.'

'Who by?'

'Probably best if you don't know. I'm going to be seeing old friends of both us from the drug trade and...'

'No, Travis, don't. Think about this.'

'It's alright. I know what I'm doing.'

'What about last night?'

'What about dumping me for Billy two years ago?'

'Ouch.'

'I don't think you feel anything.'

'You know that's not true. Don't go back, Travis. Look forward.'

'It can't be helped.'

'Stay away from my sister, please.'

'I can't promise that.'

He hangs up.

What about last night? Jesus. She drives me crazy, he thinks.

Now.

His old man.

'Hello.'

'Dad.'

'Son, how are you? Had a good win yesterday I see. Played forward I heard?'

'Yeah, coach made the call on that, and it worked a beauty. I like kicking goals.'

'Ha Ha. I know that. Why the call?'

'I'm coming to Melbourne this afternoon, get in at four.'

'What for?'

'Got a job to find some people.'

'They couldn't use locals? Think about that, Travis. Why not?'

'The guy has no contacts and...'

'In this day and age, no contacts, think about it, son. You might be dispensable.'

'Can you pick me up, terminal four car park?'

'Sure, sure, be good to see you, son.'

'I'll stay one night then get a motel, just in case.'

'Just in case. Alright. See you at four.'

'Thanks, dad.'

'Anytime, anything, son.'

Travis hangs up. It hadn't always been like that with his dad.

He calls the car rental office at the airport; says he'll pick up the car in the city office.

Babus can wait.

He rings his coach at Randwick. Two weeks maximum, he tells him. Coach is pissed off.

He packs his gear.

Should he see someone about these panic attacks? He'd had them rarely, but they had escalated since Ann died in the motel. Maybe they'd stop now he was going to find the guy who killed her.

He goes for a run, a long one. It clears his head. Gets back and checks his bags, that he has everything. He messages for an Uber. At the airport, everything goes smoothly. He sits down in 1A and breathes a sigh of relief. He doesn't buy any food or drink on the discount airlines flight. It lands on time and he's first out the door and walking quickly. He only has hand luggage. He reaches the pickup point, and his old man toots the horn of his Volvo, and Travis smiles, walks quickly to the car, and the boot pops open, and he chucks his two backpacks in, gets in the passenger door, sits, and his dad reaches over and kisses him on the cheek and Travis hugs his dad and says, 'Good to see, dad. I miss you. You know that.'

'You're here now. Work to do, but we'll relax tonight. Nice meal. Quiet night. Get you settled for this job of yours.'

'Yeah. I'm hungry now, but I can wait.

'Not sure if I'll cook, maybe get some Thai take-away. How about that? I know a good place close by.'

'Great, dad, and you, how are you?'

His dad pulls out from the kerb and drives slowly out of the airport and gets on the freeway before replying, 'I'm fine, son. Never better.'

CHAPTER THIRTY

Travis checks into a sixty-dollar-a-night motel in Abbotsford. It is old, and the room smells of a recent air-freshener blast and mothballs. A colourful bedspread was tucked into the bed, a TV and small fridge, a table and chair, a small sofa, like a million other motels all over the world. He goes into the bathroom. The shower rose is the size of a frisbee. One good thing about these old places; excellent water pressure and the big rose combination is most welcome.

He has organised to meet Johnny Tran at a massage parlour in a small side street off Victoria Street. He calls Babus, she answers, 'Travis, hi.'

'Hi, babe.'

'Where are you? You took off yesterday morning in a hurry.'

'I'm in Melbourne. I'm on a PI case.'

"Melbourne. Who hired you?'

'Some guy I never heard of. His sister is missing.'

'Not too late this time, I hope.'

'No. I'm sorry I crashed out the other night. I was exhausted.'

'You had been living pretty fast.'
'I guess.'
'When are you coming back?'
'Two weeks, tops.'
'Call me often.'
'I will. Gotta go; got to find this girl.'
'Be nice to her when you find her.'
'Always.'
He hangs up.
That is done.
He calls Katya.
No answer.

He takes his laptop with him to the car. He picks up the car Chui booked for the airport at an office in Elizabeth Street. It is a small Hyundai I30. Fast, neat, reliable. He gets in and drives the short distance to the massage parlour.

No markings are showing that it is a massage parlour, but when he gets inside it is dimly lit by a couple of small orange lamps. There is a vacant, purple, vinyl couch, and the smell hits him. Talcum powder, baby oil, body odour, male fluids.

A beautiful Viet girl at the counter and a sign beside her that has the costs laid out. Among them, $60 for half-an-hour and no doubt some extra cash for extra services. Travis smiles at the girl and says, 'I'm here to see Johnny Tran. My name is Travis.'

She smiles back at him, saying nothing but picks up a phone, hits a few buttons, and smiles at him again. Someone answers on the other end, and she talks in Vietnamese. He knows a few words here and there, but she talks fast, and Travis understands nothing. She puts the phone down, says, 'Johnny says he's busy for thirty minutes. Why don't you have a massage, on the house.'

'No, don't think I'll do that.' He does not want to get naked in the vicinity of Johnny Tran, all his defences down. 'I'll take a walk, get a coffee, come back in thirty, ok?'

'Ok, sir. I tell Johnny.'

Travis walks out.

He wanders up and down Victoria Street, smoking. Sits down on a bench and turns on the data on his smartphone. Watches the news on iView. Olsen has been arrested, suspended, and charged with corruption but out on bail. Travis doesn't know what to think. Olsen seemed like a straight shooter, but he remembers, who sends around small nuggety guys to beat people up.

He reads the email from Angelo again. The Viet guys are Binh Le and Duc Phan. They used to live in Public Housing, behind Victoria Street, Richmond. It is going to be tough finding them. Johnny seems his only hope. Ahn's sister could help. She was an ice junkie for a few years until her dad kidnapped her and put her in rehab. She and Ahn don't talk anymore and Ahn might never talk to him again if he got involved with her.

He goes back to the massage parlour, and the girl smiles when she sees him. A Caucasian guy is sitting on the purple sofa. Big guy with blond hair in a bowl cut, like a giant ten-year-old. Travis nods, the guy smiles. The girl says, 'Up the stairs, first floor, the door right at the end of the corridor. He's waiting for you.'

Travis walks up the stairs, down the tight corridor with numbered doors all along it, and knocks on the door at the end of the corridor.

'Come in,' the voice says, and Travis smiles in recognition of it, opens the door, and walks in.

Inside the door, two guys grab his arms on either side. He struggles, but they hold him tight. They're Viet guys, small and strong. Johnny sits behind a desk, smiling.

'You got a short memory, Travis.'

'Meaning.'

'Did you forget Ahn's old man hates your guts?'

'But you don't work for...'

'Alliances change, my friend. You didn't do your research.'

'I need to find two guys. That's it. Nothing more. You tell me where I can find them. Ahn's old man doesn't need to know.'

'He already knows. Me too.'

Johnny nods his head to the guy on the right of Travis. The man swings his right fist hard into Travis's face. His head snaps back. He exhales with a 'fuck'. The man hits him again and again in the face, and Travis slumps. The other guy holds him up. The first man hits hard in the middle of the forehead with his elbow. Travis wavers, like he's going to fall. The guy hits him twice in the stomach, hard. The wind gets knocked out of him, and the other guy lets him fall to the floor, and the first man kicks him in the mouth. Travis tastes blood, lots of it.

'Enough,' Johnny Tran says. 'You had enough, Travis?'

Travis says nothing, lies still, curled up in a ball to protect himself. No more blows yet.

Johnny Tran gets up from behind the desk and walks towards Travis and leans down, says, 'Relax, Travis, it's over. You go home now, get on a plane, don't fucken come back.'

Travis gets up on his knees. Johnny bends down right in his face. Travis grins and head butts him square in the forehead, grabs his hair, and head butts him again in the right eye. Johnny tries to tear himself away from Travis's grip on his hair. Travis holds him tight, rips his hair out and loses his grip. The two men and Johnny rain down blows on him from all angles. Then the three of them start kicking him from every angle. Travis curls up in a ball again on the floor and thinks, I got my shot in you, cunt, you won't forget this day. Johnny Tran streams blood from the two blows, and his head screams in pain at the hair ripped from it. If it was anyone else, he would kill them. But Travis is well-known; he will be missed. They stop the beating and leave him on the floor. Johnny tells the two men to leave.

Five minutes later the big blond guy from the entrance comes into the room and picks Travis up. Checks all his pockets. Takes the car keys out, shakes Travis who says, 'I get the message. I get the message.'

The big man helps him along the corridor, down the stairs. Travis is aching all over. The big guy leads him to his car out the front. Opens the back door. Puts Travis up against the car.

'This was a warning. You come back again, I'll beat you to death.'
Travis smiles, says, 'Go fuck yourself.'

The big blond man-child hits him hard in the face and a couple of teeth fly out, and Travis collapses, but the man holds him up, then folds him into the back seat. Slams the door. Opens the front door. Puts the keys in the ignition, says, 'Goodbye, loser,' and walks back inside.

Travis wakes up hours later his whole body, aching.

The sun is piercing his eyeballs. He tries to sit up but lies back down because it hurts like a motherfucker. He knows where he is. He remembers. He wants to get out of there quick time. He manages to sit up. Looks in the rear-view mirror at his face, opens his mouth to see where two of his teeth got knocked out. One on the bottom row, the other a few teeth along at the top left-hand side. Great. He can see a dark purple bruise on his forehead getting bigger by the second. He pushes the back door open. Gets the front door open while bent over, edges his way into the car. Keys in the ignition. Smart guys.

He starts the engine and pulls slowly away from the curb, pretty much every muscle in his body hurting. Johnny Tran working for or with Ahn's old man. He didn't see that coming. He gets back to the motel, parks out front of his room and struggles out of the car and into the room. He examines himself more closely in the bathroom mirror. Those missing teeth make him look like a loser who can't afford a dentist. The bruise continues to spread across his forehead, a couple of nicks under his right eye and some bruises under his left eye. His body aching. He rings a dentist in Collingwood, says it's an emergency. They give him an appointment for 10 am tomorrow. They can put in temporary crowns for him while they measure for the new ones.

Travis wedges the chair from under the desk to under the front door. Slides the desk and the old sofa right behind it. Anyone comes for him, he'll know. He has to get a gun he thinks. He kicks his shoes off and lies down gently on the bed. That blond guy with the bowl cut. The two Viet guys and old Johnny Tran kicking the living shit out of him. He managed to get a couple of decent head butts into Johnny. He smiles, still in the game, Travis. Still in the game. He finds some sleeping pills in his bag and takes two washed down with water and closes his eyes.

CHAPTER THIRTY-ONE

While Travis tries to sleep away the pain, Perry sits in the Preston Airbnb, smoking. Katya is in the shower. Perry and Katya haven't been partying, but Perry found a guy on a dating app. More like a Tinder app but called something different. He has to meet the guy in a couple of hours at his place.

His mobile rings. A private number, but she answers, Dylan says, 'I'm going to be staying another night in Sydney. I have to look after something important.'

'Katya and I are in Preston.'

'I know, you told me that. You told the boy about me, didn't you?'

'What boy?'

A beat.

Two beats.

Perry says, 'You mean the coloured boy?'

'Who else?'

'No, I didn't tell him anything. That boy is fine. He can't do anything.'

'Travis has been looking out for him. He's known him a while now, but suddenly he starts taking him to football games, picking him up, dropping him off.'

'I don't know anything about...'

'You do know. I'm telling you.'

'I... I don't know.'

'Travis is in Melbourne too.'

'What?'

'He's there, he's in Melbourne. I followed him to the airport.'

'Oh shit.'

'I'll call you again when I get to Melbourne. You keep Katya quiet too.'

'Yeah, yes, I will.'

Perry starts to leave to meet her date as Katya walks from the bathroom. He tells her.

'Travis is in Melbourne.'

'How do you know that?'

'I just do.'

'Oh.'

'Don't tell anyone anything about Dylan coming. Not your boyfriend, Travis, or anyone, you understand?'

'Yeah, I understand, but if he didn't do that to...'

'Be quiet, baby. Perry is taking care of everything, alright. Watch Netflix, smoke some weed, ok?'

'Ok.'

Perry leaves, Katya calls Travis, but his mobile rings out. She tries another three times with the same result. She doesn't leave a message; he'll know she rang from the mobile number. She knows Dylan is connected to Ann's death. He might not have done it, but he was involved. The cops will crucify her if they find out. She needs to placate Travis. She knows he won't stop if he thinks she knows what happened or that Dylan is coming here to Melbourne.

CHAPTER THIRTY-TWO

Travis wakes up in the middle of the night, body aching. He slides his legs off the bed onto the floor, stands a little unsteadily. His forehead hurts worse than any knock he ever had from football. He checks his mobile phone. 4.30 am. He may as well get under that frisbee shower rose. He checks his face first. The bruise is going to be clear to see to the dentist or anyone else looking at him. He'll buy a cap. He won't ring Ahn's sister in case she says no. He'll drive up to her place. She lives in Belgrave in the Dandenong Ranges about an hour and a half from Abbotsford. He showers for twenty-minutes under steaming hot water. Feels slightly better. That fucken Johnny. He still can't get over it. Aligned with Ahn's father, but he made out he knows the guys who stole the money. He stupidly made that clear. But obviously, he doesn't know where they are.

He fills the ancient kettle with water, plugs it in, turns it on. Finds the motel supplied Nescafe coffee sachets, rips open two sachets, pours them in a small cup. There is UHT milk in tiny containers. The kettle boils. He fills the cup about half-way, puts in a couple of small dobs of milk. It's like mud. He lights a cigarette, sips the strong, bitter coffee, starts to feel more like himself again, albeit with aches and pains that will take days, maybe longer, to get over. Ahn's father name is Chi Dang. Ahn told him Chi meant man of purpose. He is certainly that.

He checks his phone again. Katya rang three times yesterday afternoon while he was asleep. He has to be careful now. He is close. First the dentist, then Ahn's sister. He takes a chance, calls Katya. It is 5 am. She answers. Perry is still out on his date.

'Travis.'

'Hi Katya, it's good to hear your voice. How are you?'

'I want to go back to Sydney. I want to do what I was doing before all this happened.'

'All what?'

'You know, poor Ann.'

'Is Perry there?'

'No, he went on some Tinder date or something.'

'Has he talked about what happened at all? Who the guy with Ann was?

'I can't talk about...'

'That girl died on my fucken watch. You sent her to me. Now who the fuck is this guy? Where can I find him? Tell me now, for fuck's sake.'

'He's coming. Perry says he's coming.'

'What's his name?'

'I can't Travis. I can't,' she starts crying.

'Yes, you can. Think about Ann. I saw her body; she was cut from head to toe. Sliced to pieces with a...'

'Dylan. His name is Dylan. That's all I know.'

'I can't see you, Katya, it wouldn't be smart now, but tell me where you are.'

'I can't.'

'You can.'

She hangs up.

Travis waits until 7 am, then he calls Olsen.

'Mr Whyte. What now?'

'The killer's name is Dylan.'

'You seen the news?'

'Yeah, I know you're suspended, but that's his name. Can't you get your guys to run it through a database or something.'

'You been watching Mission Impossible, Travis?'

'I'll get his surname, alright. If I can get his name, you'll help me?'

'If you get his full name, yeah, I can help.'

'Thanks.'

Olsen hangs up.

He calls Katya. She doesn't answer. He leaves a message pleading with her to call him back.

———

Travis gets the temporary crowns. The dentist didn't ask how it happened. He did tell him it would take a week until the permanent crowns were ready. What can you do, he thinks. He gets in his car, rings Katya again.

He holds his breath.

She answers.

'Where are you, Katya?'

'Preston.'

'Preston. Whose idea was that? It doesn't matter. Where in Preston?'

She gives him the address.

'Good girl, Katya. Good girl. I'm going to get you out of this.'

'What are you going to do?'

'I don't exactly know, yet. But sit tight. Don't tell Perry that…'

'He knows you're here. He told me yesterday. He told me not to…'

The line goes dead, static, then nothing.

Did Perry hear her; did she hear her talking to him? Shit.

Does he go there now? No. This guy Dylan isn't there yet. Perry wouldn't let Travis in. He might even attack him. He would welcome that; he would beat the shit out of him. Evil fucker.

He buys a black cap at a $2 store on Victoria Street, pulls it low down on his head, gets into the near-new Hyundai, turns on the sports radio station SEN, listens to Whatley talking about AFL. Whatley pisses him off. He thinks sport should be played like in some idyllic 1950's dream of his, but he kind of likes listening so he can get angry at him, slam the dash and say 'fucken idiot.'

He drives to the Burwood Highway, wonders what the fuck he is going to say to Ahn's sister, Susie? Little Susie. The firecracker.

CHAPTER THIRTY-THREE

Travis pushes the small, fake-pearl doorbell. A chime rings inside. He waits. Hears soft footsteps, the door opens a fraction, one eye looking him over. He waits, the eye looks, he hears, 'Oh my gosh. Travis. Come in, come in.'

She is dressed in tight blue tracksuit bottoms, a black t-shirt under which her bra-free boobs are moving as she's jumping up and down.

Travis laughs.

Still the same, he thinks.

'Sit down. Sit down. Nobody ever tells me anything about you, you poor thing.'

'Susie, I'm looking for a couple of guys. Vietnamese guys into drugs. I think that...'

'What the fuck? You want me to get mixed up with drugs again. Travis, I thought you came to see me,' she says folding her arms now, looking away, acting hurt.

'I did. I did come to see you, but the reason I came to Melbourne was to find these guys. I have to do that, after that we can hang out a bit, like old times.'

'No.'

'What?'

'No. I won't help you.'

'Susie, what?'

'I'm joking. Ha Ha Ha. Joking. I'll help you, Travis. It'll be exciting, like you said, like the old days.'

Travis hopes to hell her father hasn't put someone on his tail. Jesus, what if he has, Travis thinks?

'These two Vietnamese guys, they're small-time drug dealers, maybe users too, I don't know. They used to live in the Richmond Housing Commission Flats.'

'Names,' she says, and, 'Oh, Travis, I didn't offer you a coffee. Why are you wearing that cap so low down over your pretty face? Oh, you have some cuts. Take the hat off, Travis. I can help you. Take the cap off.'

Travis takes the cap off, looks up at her.

'Oh dear, oh my gosh, come to the bathroom now, come. I have stuff to help you. It's called Arnica cream; it reduces bruising. I have some mercurochrome for those cuts. Come on. Come on. My little boy gets cuts all time.'

'You have a son?'

'A girl and a boy, but their father is a complete cunt who ran off. Don't worry. It's school holidays. They're with their ba, their grandmother.'

'Right.'

'It's perfect timing for us to go out and find these guys. Their names, Travis. You didn't tell me their names.'

'Binh Le and Duc Phan.'

'I know him. I fucken know him. Duc Phan. He's about five years older than me. He used to deal ice. I scored off him a few times when I used and yeah, he was a user, you could tell, slightly mad. He used to think he could have me, but no way, not even when I was fucked up. No Viet guys, you know that, Travis. I like white guys.'

'What about black guys?'

'Yeah, black guys too. Not Viet. It's a dad thing.'
'Glad we cleared that up, Susie. Now if...'
'I can make a few calls. I can find him.'
'Great. That's great.'
'Yes.'

Travis is overwhelmed. Susie is a whirling dervish. He can't take her to find these guys, but she won't tell him unless he does, he knows that. She's crazy. Maybe, maybe. If he can bring Ahn into it.

She starts applying the cream to his forehead softly, gently. It feels amazing. The cream is cooling. He closes his eyes for a minute as she continues, saying, 'That's better, isn't it? Aren't you glad you came to see me? That's it, close your eyes.'

She starts rubbing his chest at the same time and it feels even better. She keeps applying the cream a little bit at a time, running her hand down his chest to his stomach, his eyes still closed. She runs her hand past his stomach to his belt. He opens his eyes, and she smiles, says, 'Let me do this,' while undoing his belt. He feels kind of hypnotised, he lets her. She stops putting the cream on his forehead, unzips him, reaches in for his dick. He lets her. She holds it, gently runs her hand over the head of it, he slides down in the chair she brought in. She opens his jeans wide. For a fleeting moment he thinks about Babus. Ahn flicks through his mind. He gives in. She keeps stroking him slowly. He's a bit delirious. She strokes a little faster, gets down on her knees, takes his cock in her mouth, holds his balls, and he comes hard inside her mouth. She swallows, leans back, and he opens his eyes. She's standing up. He says, 'Sorry, sorry.'

'Who are you apologising to?' She asks, then rinses her mouth under the tap and stands up straight, says, 'I always wanted to make you come.'

He stares at her in bewilderment.

She starts laughing as she looks at him putting himself together, says, 'You enjoyed it sooo much too, didn't you?'

'Ah, yeah, come on Susie. Make those calls. Find this guy for me.'

'Alright, alright. We will, but we'll get back to that other business when we find this little cocksucker.'

'You're exhausting, Susie.'

'Moi?'

She takes her mobile from a side pocket in her tracksuit pants, stabs in the numbers. Someone answers. She starts talking rapidly in Vietnamese. She mentions Bond Street in Abbotsford, he got that much, then she continues talking quickly again, laughing and talking. Travis sits, puts the cap back on. She finishes the call, makes another and another, always speaking quickly, then one final call until she puts the mobile down.

'Well?'

'Two boys came from Sydney, started talking big-time about buying up a lot of ice and heroin. They're your boys. Not in Richmond. They're holed up in an Airbnb in Clayton.'

'They have Airbnb in Clayton? Who comes to Melbourne and stays in Clayton?'

'Parents of students at Monash Uni. Drug dealers.'

Travis laughs.

'You got the exact address?'

'I have.'

'Let's go.'

'Slow down,' she says, surprising him. 'I can't come with you. These guys are likely to have weapons. I have kids'

'Right, wait. Can you get me a handgun?'

'No. I can't do that anymore.'

'No, I get it.'

Travis thinks about what is about to happen. Lots of cash. Possibly ice-affected drugs dealers who are paranoid.

He calls his old man.

'Travis?'

'Yep. I told you why I'm here.'

'You did.'

'The guys are in Clayton. Possibly using ice. Maybe they have weapons.'

'Don't be stupid, son. No weapons. Sit on the apartment or flat or whatever it is. Take one guy, then the other. I can do this with you. I still know the game. The risks.'

'Camp in my car near their house and wait.'

'Yes, let me know when you need a break or if you need me quickly, I'll come. Where are you now?'

'Belgrave.'

'Should take you an hour to get there.'

'Yep.'

'I'll wait for your call.'

'Bye, dad.'

It is smart. His old man is smart. The waiting game with ice heads.

His mobile rings.

Olsen.

'Travis.'

'Yeah, what's up.'

'You probably haven't heard. Not in the media, yet.'

'What isn't?'

'The young Aboriginal boy, Paul.'

'Leave him out of this.'

'He was found this morning in his squat.'

'Found?'

'He's dead, Travis. Bound and gagged. Cut to pieces, like Ann.'

'Holy shit. No. No fucking way. Dylan killed him; he must have. That boy was starting to take off, his life was getting better.'

'Travis, you can't ex...'

'You sure about this?'

'You know how many times I've made calls like this?'

'Yeah.'

'I have to go, Travis.'

'Yeah, right.'

'You know what this means?'
'What?'
'You're next. He's coming for you.'
'He always was.'
'I know why you're in Melbourne.'
Travis hangs up.
Fuck Olsen.
He wants something.
That boy.
Kicked a few goals, he said.
'Shit. Shit. Fuck!'

Susie looks at his face, tears well up in his eyes. She comes and sits next to him, puts her arm around him, kisses him lightly on the side of his head.

Rocks him a bit.

CHAPTER THIRTY-FOUR

As Travis drives to the Airbnb in Clayton, Katya smokes another joint trying to obliterate the memory of Ann. Hiding. The rest of her life could be like this. Travis would come for her, eventually, even if she didn't tell him when Dylan was coming.

She hears the key in the front door, wipes some damp sweat of her forehead. Turns the TV on. Maybe Perry will go straight to bed after being out all night. Perry comes into the lounge, puts her car keys on the glass coffee table, looks at Katya, says, 'You're out of it. You're sweating. What's wrong? What are you worried about?'

'Nothing. Nothing.'

'Tell me the truth,' Perry says, walking across and shaking her. 'Tell me the truth.'

'I'm scared. I'm scared,' she says and starts crying. 'What if Dylan... I don't know, what if... I told Travis. I told him where we are.'

'You stupid fucken bitch. Give me your mobile. Give it to me now. Give it.'

Perry reaches down, grabs it out of her hand. Opens it up, takes the sim card out, puts it in the ashtray. Lights it on fire with a small blue Bic lighter. It melts into nothing.

'No more mobile for you. Do you want to die? Do you want Travis to die? You know he can do it. I'm telling you, if Dylan finds out you spoke to Travis, told him where we are. Fuck. Pack your shit. Pack your shit, now. We're leaving.'

CHAPTER THIRTY-FIVE

Travis drives by the house in Clayton where the two guys are supposedly holed up. It's a weatherboard house in a street mostly of small single-fronted houses and 1970's blocks of units and — because the front lawns aren't mowed — rubbish bins aren't brought in. He figures they're mostly rented. The house is on a street a few blocks from the Clayton Shopping Plaza on Centre Road. It's cold; rain is falling gently on his hired Hyundai. Susie is cool; she knows so many people. He is sure she has the right guys. Back when he was using, she was the wild child, and everybody loved her. Still wild, but no drugs now.

The streets around here are wide. Clayton is hemmed in by, if not freeways, then busy main roads all around it. He figures the street is probably inhabited by students, young shared-house fuckwits, possibly young families, single males in small studio units, all struggling a bit with finances. He's guessing all this, just running shit through his brain while he waits. The Hyundai is parked about seventy metres from the house. He waits, anxious. His chest starts getting tight, hard to breathe. This shit again, he thinks. He gets out of the car and crouches down on his haunches. That Aboriginal boy killed, sliced up, is in his head and he can't get rid of the image. He tries to suck in breath after breath, but he can't. His hearts races. His chest beats like a snare drum. He coughs and finally gets some air in his lungs. The rain gets heavier; no-one is out in the street. He puts his hand across his chest trying to breathe in and out and slowly, slowly, he can breathe again.

When is this shit going to stop, he thinks as he gets back in the front seat and waits. He can see the house. An old Datsun sedan parked in the drive. One of the few houses to have a driveway. He wants to smoke but thinks it might give him away. It is 1 pm, still no-one in the street, no curtains opening to check him out. I'm next in line according to Olsen. Travis knows it. Olsen put the wind up him though. This job, then Katya. Go get her out of danger. He hated that their relationship was tenuous at best now. She can't trust him; he can't trust her. They had been so close when he worked in the motel. He looked out for her and she him, but the murder had changed all that. She has chosen her side and it is Perry, but he can't let her be entrapped by him with the threat of violence from Dylan or even Perry himself. He rings her. The number doesn't connect. Tries again. What the hell, he thinks. Tries her again. There's not even a message of any kind, a few short beeps then nothing. Her mobile... he can't think straight for a few minutes. He could give the Preston address to Olsen, but he doesn't want Katya too, um... Wait he thinks. Wait.

The front door of the house opens. An Asian guy in blue jeans, a black puffy jacket, walks out, gets in the car, starts it up, backs down the drive, then waits for a few minutes before driving off. Is this it? Is this his chance now? He gets out of the car, walks quickly along the street in the rain. He has no rain jacket, and it's getting heavy; the air is much colder than it was this morning.

He walks past the house then quickly turns back, runs down the left-hand side of the driveway. He comes to a tall wire gate, a few feet taller than him, with a padlock on it. He climbs over it as quietly as possible, drops down on the other side, and thinks, shit, dog, but it's quiet. No dog. Not outside anyhow. He walks slowly along the side of the house crouched below window level. He looks in the first window; a backpack on a bed, nothing else. He hears music. Jagged punkish rock. He goes to the second window at the back of the house. He stands up slowly to slightly above window level, looks in the window. It is the kitchen.

There's a Vietnamese guy, about thirty. Music is pumping from a small boom box, loud, edgy. The Viet guy rocks out, dancing jerkily about like he's in the middle of a mosh pit. He turns sharply, sees Travis at the window. Fuck. Stops. Runs to a drawer, grabs a knife and charges through the kitchen to the back door.

Travis is frozen. What the fuck, he thinks, what now? He holds his ground, waits for the Viet guy to come. The man walks quickly around the corner of the house to the side passage, sees Travis, feet planted waiting, says, 'Who the fuck? What are you doing here? Fuck off. Fuck off.'

He keeps walking at Travis with the knife in his right hand held out in front of him, ready to strike. Travis lets him come in close, to within a foot, the man high on ice, lunges super-fast, cuts Travis on his left forearm, blood runs. Travis backs up but only a small way. The man lunges again, but Travis steps inside him and slams the palm of his hand into the underside of the man's nose. Blood explodes. The knife drops to the ground. Travis kicks him in the balls, once, twice, three times. The man is down on his knees. Travis picks up the knife as he hears the car come into the drive. He runs to the back door, opens it, quickly goes inside, locks the door.

The car door slams, and the man walks up the short path to the small concrete veranda and knocks on the door. Shit. He doesn't have a key. How could he not have a key, Travis thinks. Must have been a signal, because he hears the front door open. Travis runs to the front of the house. The man is coming in the door, Travis runs straight at him, tackles him to the ground, brings the knife up, holds it at the man's throat.

'Don't say anything. Keep your mouth shut.' Blood oozes from the cut on his forearm.

The second Viet guy, says, 'Who are you? You want the money? I can give you ten thousand. You go away. Tell them you couldn't find us.' This guy is straight, not high.

Travis says, 'Get up. Get up.'

He takes the knife from his throat. The guy stands up. Travis has the man's arm held tight. He is smaller than Travis but wiry, strong. Travis has the knife by his side in the other hand. The man violently jerks back, slams his boot into Travis' foot hard. Travis backs away in pain. The man comes at him swinging fists, left and right, fast combinations, some landing, others missing. The man is super-fast like his friend. Travis backs up. The man comes in. Travis cuts him down the side of his face. The guy stops immediately, feels his face, the blood pouring out from the cut on his fleshy cheek. Travis grabs him by the hair, drags him into the first bedroom where he saw the backpack. Throws him to the ground, kicks him twice in the face and breaks some teeth. Kicks him twice more in the balls.

Could it be this easy? He unzips the backpack as he hears the back door being assaulted by the other Viet guy. Nothing. He looks in the cupboard, under the bed. The Viet man is moaning, crying. Travis takes the key from the inside of the door and locks the man in the bedroom. He goes to the next bedroom. Nothing on the bed. He looks in the closet. Three or four shirts hung up, an old suit jacket. He looks under the bed. Nothing.

He hears a window smash; the other Viet man trying to break back into the house. This is not the patience his old man wanted him to show. He walks down the short hallway to the lounge room, which faces the street. Looks under the sofa, under the two armchairs. Nothing. Where is it? What have they done with it? He goes to the second bedroom again. Pulls back the doona. Nothing. There are draws in the base of the bed. He pulls them out onto the floor. The other man. Where is he? Has he broken in yet? He looks into the base of the bed. A bag. Another backpack. An orange backpack. He has to tip the bed up. The backpack is larger than normal. It's heavy, full of something inside. He lays it flat, quickly unzips it. There it is. The cash packed tight.

The first guy has broken in through the kitchen window, blood covers his face. He is breathing heavily as he runs at Travis saying, 'You cunt! You...'

Travis says, 'Come on then cunt. You want to get cut.'

The man stops. Travis opens the front door, says, 'Stay the fuck where you are.'

He closes the door. Puts the knife into the backpack, walks quickly to his car. Opens the driver side door, throws the money in, smiling, almost laughing, but the noise, the cops might come. He gets in the car, starts it, drives fast down the street. The men are on the veranda watching him go. Travis can't help himself; he toots the horn as they look at him speed away. He needs to bandage his arm. He'll cover it up, stop at a chemist. He will take the car back to Hertz. They have number plates now, but they're on their own. They don't seem to be aligned with anyone; this is what Angelo's email told him also. They were small-time guys who took a risk that paid off, then didn't. Even if they have the plates. What can they do? Nothing. It's done. He won, he thinks, at last. He might upgrade the tape deck in the Millennium Falcon to a CD player.

Then he thinks about the Aboriginal boy, Paul. If it had been anything like Ann in the room at the motel, it would have been an awful death, slashed here and there all over his young, fit body.

I kicked a few goals.

CHAPTER THIRTY-SIX

Andy Chui picks up his mobile, says, 'Travis.'

'I have the money, but I can't bring it back. I have some business here.'

'Angelo will take the first available flight. He stays at the Sheraton, opposite the Treasury Gardens. I'll book two rooms. Get out of your cur...'

'I'm checked out now. I'll Uber to the Sheraton. I'm at Hertz on Elizabeth Street.'

'Any problems?'

'A shit fight to be honest. I need to see a doctor, get some stitches. There's a guy in Reservoir will do it. One of them was high on ice, and they were both angry, but yeah, I don't think you'll have to worry about them. Ahn's father's friends gave me a working over the first night, as a warning.'

'You earned your cash. Get back to Sydney as soon as you can. You work for me now.'

The lines goes dead.

Like fuck I do, thinks Travis.

He rang Ahn quickly to get the doctor onside. He was a friend of her father. She did it.

The doctor stitches up his wounds. They don't speak. Her father would be furious if he knew. Too bad. The doctor knows this. He won't say anything.

He checks into the Sheraton. The room has already been paid for. The orange backpack sits like a trophy on the red sofa. He waits. Then he orders room service. Tells reception he wants no calls. Still not done yet. After the burger, fries, and milkshake arrive, he pushes the sofa up against the door, the desk behind it, lies down. The room landline rings.

'What?'

'Mr Whyte, there's a gift left for you at reception. Do you want the porter to bring it up.'

'Yes.'

He shifts the sofa and desk back.

A knock on the door. There's a fisheye. He looks through it. The porter with a basket of flowers. He opens the door. The porter hands him the basket of flowers. Travis tips him with a twenty, closes the door. Puts the sofa and desk back. There is a card. A postcard of Flinders Street Station. A handwritten note.

Don't come back. Signed *Johnny Tran.*

At what point did they follow him? Most likely from the time he checked out of the motel. If they had been in Clayton, he would have known. It was too much money not to have a stab at. Susie's connections were better than her old man. More street level.

Travis closes his eyes and waits.

CHAPTER THIRTY-SEVEN

Angelo picked up the cash. He had Wicky from the gambling club with him. Angelo wasn't in a talking mood. Travis wonders if he was pissed off about him walking out of the casino job after he had helped set it up for him. Wicky said they would drive back to Melbourne. Too much cash for the airport domestic security guys to let pass without questions.

Travis is up at 7 am. He eats big from the free buffet breakfast. Sausages, eggs, bacon, two croissant, orange juice, two coffees, a third coffee as take-away that he drinks while smoking and driving to Preston in a new BMW, hired by Angelo, as a gift for the rest of his stay. This time from Avis. He can drive it back to Melbourne or leave it at the airport. Angelo didn't ask why he was staying on in Melbourne.

Travis arrives at the block of units on Cooma Street, Preston. He hits three or four buttons on the intercom. Someone answers, he says, 'Postman with a package.'

The buzzer sounds, and he enters. Number ten is on the third floor. He runs up the stairs not sure what he's going to do. Would

Dylan, or whatever his real name is, be there? It might be like Clayton. A shit-fight. As he nears the top stairs, he slows down, reaches the third floor. Stops. Does some breathing. Slow in and out. Hand across his chest, breathing in and out. He doesn't want a panic attack now or ever again. He finds the door, knocks as loudly as can. Nothing. He knocks again. Waits. Nothing. He knocks again. The guy from number nine pokes his head out, says, 'They've gone.'

'Who?'

'The girls.'

'Where'd they go?'

'Are you some...'

'I'm a private investigator. They stole a lot of money. My job is to get it back.'

'Oh.'

'Was there any noise, any shouting?'

'Something about one of the girls' mobile. *No phone for you. Do you want to get killed? Get Mavis killed.*'

'Travis?'

'Yeah, maybe it was Travis.'

'When?'

'This morning.'

'You know where they went?'

'No.'

Travis believes him.

Why would he lie?

'Right, thanks, mate. Sorry to bother you.'

'No bother for you, sir,' and Travis notices a cheeky smile. The guy is hitting on him.

'Have to go, thanks again.'

He walks quickly away back down the stairs.

He calls Airbnb, finding the number to speak to a human was hard enough, but now they stonewall him. Private, sorry, can't give out any details.

'This person is a friend of mine; we were supposed to meet and...'
'I'm sorry, sir, but I...'
'Go fuck yourself.'
He calls Olsen.
'Travis, this is getting to be a thing.'
'I know you don't like me, but I need some details from Airbnb. Perry the pimp dealer I told you about. He was staying in Preston but checked out. I need a contact number. Maybe you can chase credit card details or...'
'Whoa, whoa. Buddy. I'm on the outer. Suspended.'
'But you said...'
'A name, Travis. I can maybe help you if you give me a name.'
'I know the Airbnb they stayed in. They're no longer there. Maybe you can find out what name they checked in under.'
'I can't do anything like that. I may have a friend in the force who could run me a name, but I'm on the outer. My friends in the force are no longer my friends. Dumped me like a load of trash at the tip. You know that feeling, don't you, Travis? Being on the outer.'
'I'm sorry, Olsen. I don't know the circumstances. I hope you're clean or...'
The line went dead.
Travis does know the feeling.
His mobile rings. A number he doesn't recognise.
'Hello.'
'Travis Whyte?'
'Who wants to know?'
'My name is Geoff Horsley.'
'And?'
'You're the guy who found Billy Madison. You do work for Andy Chui.'
'Yes,'
'I want to hire you. My daughter went missing three days ago. She was in Melbourne on holiday with her best friend. She and her friend didn't come back.'

'You want me to find her?'

'Yes.'

'What are the police doing?'

'Nothing. She's nineteen.'

'I'm in Melbourne now as it happens.'

'You'll do it.'

'I'm not good on the phone. I'll give you my email address, you talk to your wife or other friends or siblings, get all the details you can about the trip. Who her friend is and her mobile number, where they were booked in to stay, flight details, people who might have met them at the airport. I want their Facebook, Twitter, Instagram accounts. That new one, TikTok, if they're on it. Anything you can think of. Where they planned to go? My guess is there'll be lots of photos and postings on social media, then they'll stop. My job will be to find out when and why they stop? Then, I can find her.'

'Oh, Jesus. Oh, thanks. How much is....'

'Three hundred a day plus expenses, meaning motel costs, food, drink, entry into shithole nightclubs and other places. You'll get an invoice.'

'I understand, thanks. Thanks for taking the job.'

'What's her full name and age and her friend? I need that now.'

'Jenny Hampton. Nineteen. That's my daughter. The other girl is Missy Murrihy. She's the same age.'

'Thanks, I'll be in touch. Any new information you put it in the email. If you think something's urgent, you ring me. Only if it's urgent.'

'Thanks, I will.'

'Goodbye, Mr Hampton.'

Jesus, life is strange, Travis thinks. You find a dead guy who is kind of well known, work for a famous rich guy. People start calling you. He likes it.

Travis looks up at the block of units, sees they each have a small balcony. He walks back upstairs to the apartment on Cooma Street. The Airbnb didn't even know they'd left. Maybe they left something behind. He takes his laptop out of the boot. He'll go through Jenny and Missy's Facebook, Instagram, and other accounts in the flat. Maybe the guy next door would make him a coffee.

CHAPTER THIRTY-EIGHT

He knocks on the door of the guy next door, and he opens the door looking bewildered as Travis says, 'Any chance I could climb over your balcony, try and get into the flat next door where they were? I might be able to find something they left behind, point me to where they are.'

'Ah, I don't know. Yeah, I guess it would be alright.'

He opens the door wide. Travis walks in. It's a small neat flat. Couch, one armchair, big screen TV, small kitchenette, tidy, nothing out on the benches.'

'I'm Micky,' the guy says, puts out his hand. Travis shakes his hand, the guy looks at him directly in the eyes.

Travis says, 'I'll check that balcony.'

He walks through the lounge, opens the door, looks to his right. It's an easy climb over, and when he gets there the door is not even closed. He waves to his new friend, says, 'Bingo. Open,' pointing to the door.

He walks into the lounge. It's messy, empty cigarette packets on the coffee table. Used coffee mugs, one of them with the symbol of the Carlton Football Club, who were going to be Travis's best outcome on draft night three years ago. There's a box of matches and playing cards. The couch has lifestyle magazines thrown on it. He picks them up, shakes them out. Nothing. Nothing in the dirty kitchen except more used mugs, dirty plates, and pots and pans. He feels like sweeping it all onto the ground, picking up a mug, throwing it at the TV. These two, Perry and Katya, they started everything. He would try and protect Katya. Paul is dead. He wonders for a moment about the funeral then changes his mind. It was only once Paul started hanging out with Travis that his life was taken. Dylan or whatever the fuck his real name is had followed them both. Stalked and killed the boy. The boy looked strong. Travis figures Dylan drugged him first.

He goes to the first bedroom. Unmade bed with an ashtray in the middle of it, ash spilled on the sheets. Black bra left behind on the back of a chair. He opens the chest-of-drawers. Goes through each drawer. Nothing. His mind flicks to Ahn. How was she doing with Farez? He didn't talk about it with Angelo. There wasn't any time with Ahn. He needed the doctor, fast. He was in too much of a hurry to get back to Melbourne. Babus would expect him to call.

He goes to the closet, slides back the mirrored door, stares at emptiness. Goes to the ensuite. Lipstick stains on the bench. A used razor in the sink. He knows that Katya shaves her legs. He opens the cabinet. A box of tampons. Cotton buds. They left in a bit of a hurry. Took the big stuff. He goes to the second bedroom feeling defeated. Looks in the closet. Zero. Under the bed. Under the sheets. No chest-of-drawers in here but a small luggage rack. He turns around in a three-sixty arc, finds nothing in his vision that can help him.

He goes back to the first bedroom. Opens the closet again, runs his hand along the top shelf. Finds something thin, like cardboard, a card. A business card for an Uber driver. Raj Singh. He didn't know they had individual cards. Maybe old Raj was an innovator or liked his return business without going through the Uber machine. Hopefully, it was left by Perry and not some other prior guest. Katya would never keep anything like that. Everything about her is unplanned.

He rings the mobile number on the card.

'Raj speaking.'

'I need an Uber booking.'

'Do I know you?'

'Not me but a couple of friends of mine used you. They gave me the number from the card you gave them.'

'Who was it?'

'Two girls staying at an Airbnb in Preston.'

'From Adelaide, yes I remember. One girl was fun, the other a bit sad, I...'

'Yeah, that's them, from Adelaide.'

Or Sydney, Travis thought. Perry, deflecting everything away.

'The thing is, I lost contact with them after they left Preston. I lived a few floors down. We hooked up a few times. I want to get together with them again. Did you pick them up this morning?'

'Yeah, took them across the city to St Kilda.'

'Can you pick me up in an hour and take me there?'

'Sure thing. Same address in Preston.'

'Yes.'

'I had a deal with those girls I...'

'Give me the same deal whatever it is. It's cool. You want to make some real cash.'

'Yeah, see you in an hour.'

Travis lets out a sigh. A release of tension. Will Dylan be with them? Can it end this quickly?

He opens his laptop. Checks out the emails from the father of the missing girl. Nothing about where they went to school together. He fires back an email asking for the information. Also, a list of best friends. A shortlist, maybe three or four people for each girl. If you don't know, ask their siblings, he wrote, ask your wife, ask the friends you do know. It's important.

He looks at the Facebook page of Jenny, checks all posts from the previous week. She announced she had arrived in Melbourne, but there was nothing after that. He tried Missy. The girls looked like each other. He guessed it was a thing. They were both blond and pretty with short hair like fashion models from the '60s. He checked Missy's posts; it showed a selfie at Tullamarine on arrival. Also, one of the girl's getting in an Uber outside the Espy Hotel. Jenny and Missy both in black jeans, black skivvies, shining short blond hair. They both looked like models, he thought again. There were no more photos or posts.

He went to Instagram, and the girls were all over it for a week, posting photos from nightclubs, pubs, daytime shots at Chapel Street, Bridge Road, Smith Street, and Chadstone Shopping Centre. If there was a predator though it would most likely be at the gigs or the clubs. He studied the photos closely while waiting for the email from the father. He also sent his bank account details for payment. A week upfront, please.

Repeated shots of the girls at The Tunnel Nightclub in Flinders Lane. He counted they were there five times including a Monday and Tuesday night. The shots were taken in the roped-off queue, which was the same as the roped-off entrance to Angels where he had been to look for Billy Madison. The girls striking poses with different guys. One or two guys popped up repeatedly both in the queue and inside the club. One was with them on a shopping trip in Smith Street, where the wholesale stores were sometimes side by side. He had neck tattoos, no big deal nowadays, not scary, sexy if anything. His arms around both girls, all laughing. Smith Street has great bars and cafés. Brunswick Street is more fashionable, but Smith Street still has some edge to it that Brunswick Street doesn't. He will take the Uber and make his play. Should he have got the address from the rogue Uber guy? He might not have given it; he might think he'd be losing fares. Why give some guy the address when he can make the trip, get a fare? Travis didn't want to fuck with the guy. He was the only link to Perry and Katya.

The girls aren't on twitter. He has their email addresses but no password. He wonders about getting the passwords. Ahn knew this whiz kid in Sydney who sometimes did illegal work for her boss, Pete Rose. He should call her, anyway, but the Uber was twenty minutes late. He rings Raj, the Uber guy.

'I can't take you there, man. I asked the girls about it, they said you were trouble.'

'What? What did you say?'

'You heard me.'

'Oh, oh, is that right? Well, how about this? How about I report your ass to Uber? Who you are currently ripping off by taking cash jobs. How do you feel about that? I have your little business card with your number on...'

'Alright, alright. But I can't pick you up.'

'Address.'

'Cosmopolitan Motel.'

'If this is wrong. I'll find you. I have your number. I know what type of car you drive.'

'It's the address I dropped them at. I gotta go. Nice talking to you.'

'Thanks, Raj, you're a prince, you know that.'

The line went dead.

Travis will drive the BM there. He has the room at the Sheraton for one more night. If he could swing it, he would try and lose Johnny Tran's tail on him after he left the Sheraton. He knew a motel behind Chapel Street, not on the main drag but further away over Dandenong Road towards St Kilda. He rang them. They told him rooms were $160 per night. That was value for the area. They have a secure car park with code entry to keep the riff-raff out. He has a paying job again.

It would take him about thirty to forty minutes to drive back across town from north to south over the Yarra River to St Kilda.

He makes a detour to Collingwood, to a small pawn store on Smith Street. Tells the guy behind the counter what he wants. The guy behind the counter is big and ugly, with a huge, bulbous nose that looks like it has been broken a few times. He has acne on his chin even though he looks to be in his forties. An awful comb over haircut. Sits on a high stool.

'Can't help you,' he says.

'How much?' Travis asks.

'Three-hundred.'

'You are...' but he shrugs his shoulders He has cash. He needs it.

He hands over the cash, and the big guy goes out the back and comes back with a blue, plastic, reusable shopping bag. He hands it to Travis who feels the weight and smiles. An old-fashioned sap. A metal pipe encased in rubber.

Serious shit.

He drives along Punt Road through heavy traffic. Perry and Katya are in the Cosmopolitan Hotel on Carlisle Street. It sits diagonally across from the sex shop on the corner of Acland and Carlisle Street. How's he going to play this? How is he going to get their room number?

He drives along Carlisle Street, straight into the car park of the hotel. Finds a spot at the back where he can see all the rooms. Waits. Hears a knock on the back of the car. Johnny Tran is in the rear vision mirror. The big blond guy with the bowl cut who punched him out, outside the massage parlour stands in front of him. Travis looks back in the rear vision. The two Viet guys from the parlour have replaced Johnny Tran who is now at the driver's side window and knocking gently, smiling. Travis takes the automatic window on the BM down a notch.

'What can I do for you, Johnny?'

'Where's the cash?'

'On the way to Sydney or already there is my best guess. I took possession and returned the cash to its owner.'

'Bullshit.'

Travis looks up at the balcony. It's fucken Katya. She sees him. Does she recognise him through the tinted windscreen? Impossible, but she sees the men surrounding the car and ducks into her room. Three along from the fire stairs. He has them.

He starts the car and accelerates straight at the blond guy who jumps onto the bonnet, tries to grip on something that isn't there, gets thrown to the left. Travis puts his foot down further, hits Carlisle Street fast. A blue muscle car immediately gets on his tail. His mobile rings at the same time. He steers with one hand and accelerates away from the muscle car, puts his left-hand blinker on but cuts across the lane and turns right onto Barkly Street. The muscle car cuts seriously late across two lanes and follows him grunting loudly. He turns left into a side street at the 7-11 store. Guns it fast. But the muscle car reaches him, rams into him as he drives along, he turns sharply left, then hard right back onto Carlisle, across the Nepean Highway, then fast left onto Chapel Street. The muscle car loses its grip. The BM is more agile; he drives fast but another car. A small bright green car with a thumping engine comes up alongside him. Johnny Tran waving him down. He pulls over into a side street off Chapel Street, near the hotel he booked.

Jumps out of the car as the two Viet gangsters come at him. He swings the sap hard, takes out the first one with a blow across the face, swings it backhand into the ear of the other man and stuns him. The fat blond guy is probably still down at the motel. Johnny Tran gets out. Travis notices the bruising on his face. This could be about honour for the headbutt the other day. He says, 'Think you can take me, Johnny?'

Johnny Tran hesitates. The first muscle car comes drumming loudly around the corner. Travis turns, runs hard down a laneway, sprints as fast as he can. Jumps a fence, finds no dog. Sits and waits. Hears the men running up and down the lane. He keeps moving through the backyard of the house to a white side gate, which he unhooks and walks down a side passage out into the street. The hotel he booked is a five-minute sprint away. He goes for it. Hears nothing coming from behind, keeps running. Their voices fade away. He sits out the front of the hotel reception area behind a small hedge. Gets his breath back. Not bad, he thinks. I have Perry and Katya's room number. I'll leave the BM. Ring Avis, tell them it broke down. Hopefully, the laptop will still be there. If not, there's nothing private on it. No account number; no passwords to anything important.

He walks into the reception office and checks in.

CHAPTER THIRTY-NINE

Two hours later he feels composed enough to go back to the Cosmopolitan. He rings Avis, tells them his story. Asks them to keep the laptop. It is under the front passenger seat. The fact that he left it might convince Johnny Tran not to search. Tran would hope the cash was there, but surely after everything Tran wouldn't think he'd leave 300K in the boot of the BM. Tran would think Travis had gone to the Cosmopolitan to try and lose him, not for Katya and Perry. Would he know about those two? Unlikely.

He calls an Uber, waits in the same spot behind the hedge in front of reception. The Uber toots the horn on arrival. Travis gets into the back seat. The Indian driver nods at him but doesn't say anything, takes off fast. Travis has given the Galleon Café as his destination; it is a hundred metres from the Cosmopolitan on the opposite side of the road. The Uber driver pops the door lock and nods at him again. Travis gets out. Nobody talks to fucken anybody anymore, he thinks. It is 5 pm, he goes inside and orders a takeaway latte, waits. How will he do this? The coffee comes. He goes outside, sits at an empty table, lights a cigarette. His mind goes back to the Cross Motel, standing on the stoop out the front, waiting for the cops, Olsen and his sidekick turning up, pretty matey with him but hard too. The grilling in the police station. Olsen sending someone around to bash him because he didn't like him; didn't like that he had information about Ann's death. His mind stops wandering. He watches the Hotel entrance.

Quiet.

He lights another cigarette, drinks the rest of the coffee. It is good. Strong and bitter without having to ask for it to be strong. Melbourne does coffee. It just does. He stubs out the cigarette, crosses the road, walks into the Cosmopolitan car park looking all around. He takes the back stairs in the far corner of the car park. The reception area faces the street. He walks up the fire escape stairs, onto the second-floor balcony where he had seen Katya. There is a housekeeping trolley outside a room five doors down. Katya is in a room three doors down from the fire escape. He goes straight to it, turns the handle of the door as the housemaid pops her head out. The handle doesn't give. The housemaid watches him.

'Forget your key, sir?' She asks in an Irish accent.

'Yeah, that's right. I forgot it.'

'I'll let you in.'

'Thanks, love.'

The door swings inwards. On the couch sits Katya with a needle stuck in her left arm, face ashen white. Travis spews up on the floor right in front of himself. The housemaid screams, 'Jaysus! Shit! Shit.'

Travis goes to Katya, grabs her hand. It is cold. Cold and damp. He feels for her pulse. Nothing. He calls an ambulance. Shit. He puts his arm around her, stares at the needle in her arm. The housemaid looks at him in horror.

'Call the police,' he says.

She stares at him.

'Call the fucken police!'

His mobile rings, Jenny's father. Travis answers, 'Hello.'

'Travis, I got a call from her a few minutes ago.'

'She alright?'

'No. She said something like, *they won't let us go. They won't let us go.* Then nothing. I tried to call back. Nothing happens. No voice mail. Nothing.'

'I'm onto it. I'm meeting with the police soon. I'll get her. I promise I'll get her and bring her home.'

He will do everything to get her back. He will go all the way.

CHAPTER FORTY

As Travis waits for the police, Dylan and Perry are in Richmond carrying on as though nothing has happened. Dylan decided that Katya, like Paul, was no longer worth the risk. She ran her mouth off too much and was clearly to him a bit of a mess. So, he gave her the hotshot. Perry said nothing but continued on in his unconscionable way.

They are staying at a two-bedroom Airbnb, but this one is upmarket on a side street off Church Street near St Kevin's College private school. Dylan has been to a private school in the eastern suburbs of Sydney, in Rose Bay. Then went to the University of New South Wales and got a degree in psychology. His parents died, and he inherited everything. He didn't work. Perry had left a Mount Druitt high school in Western Sydney when he was fourteen and gravitated to King Cross where he began a life of deceit that continued unabated now, only Dylan has money, class, and viciousness. A combination Perry hasn't seen before.

Dylan is dressed in bone-coloured chinos, a light blue Country Road shirt, and a black blazer, he says to Perry, 'We're going out tonight. There's a club in Flinders Lane, The Tunnel.'

'What time?'

'Not until late, maybe midnight or one or two AM. I'm going shopping. You want to come?'

'No.'

Perry thinks he will get Dylan drunk, slip a sleeping pill or some ketamine in his drink. But he doesn't know what to do after that. He needs to be able to blackmail him into giving him a lot of money, and he has the money. Enough Perry believes that would see him never need to run scams on people anymore. No more living day to day or week to week at best.

Perry couldn't see any way in. His parents were dead, and he didn't have any other relatives. He was only, Perry thought, twenty-eight or nine. Dylan had picked up Perry one night from a Kings Cross pick-up spot near the infamous wall and taken him to his Rose Bay mansion, tied him up and fucked him. Afterwards, he had been quiet as a kitten. That was when Perry thought the young Aboriginal boy, Paul, might please Dylan. Might please them both. Maybe that was the way in. Get him to confess to the killing of Paul, Ann, and Katya. Get it on tape.

CHAPTER FORTY-ONE

IT IS LATE. TRAVIS IS IN AN INTERROGATION ROOM AT THE St Kilda Police station on Chapel Street, East St Kilda with Detective Lois Baldock. He has already given his statement. It is clear he isn't the murderer, and the cops haven't yet made it known to the press or public. They weren't even calling it a murder; not yet, if ever. A hooker from Sydney with no family or friends takes too much heroin and is found dead in a St Kilda Motel. Who gives a fuck? Unless the guy who finds her is Travis Whyte, who was working in the Cross Motel when Ann was killed.

The Detective says to Travis, 'You can go now, Mr Whyte, thank you for your help.'

He stands up. Says to her, 'Will you be looking after...'

'I believe what you told me, Mr Whyte. I know your history also. It's Victoria. We're AFL mad and even if we're not, we can't escape it, and yours was a big story, then you slunk out of town, now you're back. A girl is dead. You found Billy Madison dead. An Aboriginal boy you knew is dead.'

'Katya, her name was Katya and the boy, his name was Paul. And it's the same guy, I told you. His name is Dylan. He'll be with a man, a crossdresser, who looks like a girl, name is Perry.'

'We'll find them, Mr Whyte.'

'But...'

'Thank you, Mr Whyte. As I said, you are not under any suspicion for any wrongdoing here, but if I were you, I wouldn't be giving Mr Olsen's name as a reference too often. He's a bit tainted, love.'

She is of medium height with blond hair, dressed in a tight black suit, a bun on top of her head, pretty, still young-looking, but to be a DI she had to be over thirty-five, he reckoned.

'Thanks for the advice,' Travis says. 'You fancy getting a drink?'

'No.'

'I've got another case. Two missing girls. What can you tell me about the Tunnel Nightclub?'

'I've got work to do, Mr Whyte.'

'Can I ask you? Can I show you a photo and you tell me if you know this man?'

'Jesus, Whyte, alright.'

He shows her the picture of the guy with tatts on his neck and arms at The Tunnel and the clearer photo of them at Smith Street. She looks closely at it. Smiles.

'That's Yevgeny Turgenev. He's the son of a well-known Russian businessman. He doesn't have any form though. He goes to Melbourne University. Not taking over the family business. But that tattoo on the right side of his neck, it is a Russian gangster tattoo. The eight-pointed star denotes a high ranking thief. But you get one of those tattoos and the wrong guy sees it. Russian or other. Might be trouble.'

She looks straight at him, smiling.

'Unless your dad is a prominent Russian businessman.'

'Very good, Mr Whyte. I might take you up on that drink another time.'

'These missing girls, they...'

'You get in trouble again, Mr Whyte, and...'

'I'm leaving.'

She hands him her business card. He smiles. She opens the door, walks him out. He turns to face her outside on Chapel Street, she says, 'Goodnight, Travis. Stay out of trouble.'

CHAPTER FORTY-TWO

Travis catches an Uber into the city. The Tunnel is near the corner of Flinders Lane and Elizabeth Street. Travis gets out at the corner of Flinders Lane and Swanston, walks slowly down Flinders Lane. The rain has started. Travis can see his breath, but he's under the shop fronts, not getting wet. He'll try to play it differently to The Angel, be more respectful, no hard man shit. It's midnight. He joins the queue. He watches the doormen. No bitches this time. There are three of them. Two guys in all black are almost identical in everything they do; the way they act. Tight hard bicep muscles under their inexpensive black suits. Bull necks. He thinks of Olsen, but these guys are in a different game. The third guy runs everything, also in a black suit, but the twins have short black hair, and he has shoulder-length blond hair.

Travis notices though that the bigger of the two with short black hair is more friendly; he's not checking how they dress — he's smiling, happy, greeting people he knows with pats on the back, kisses on the cheek for the girls — where the other two are standoffish.

When he reaches the front, he goes to the friendly guy, smiles at him, says, 'Hey, man.'

'Hey,' the big guy says.

Travis says, 'Mate, I'm a PI up from Sydney, looking for some missing girls.'

He flashes his ID at the guy, who takes it in his hand.

'Travis Whyte. I know that name.'

'Yeah, two blond girls, they were seen here all week, this past week. Here.'

He shows the big guy the photos outside the club, the photo on Smith Street with Yevgeny. The guy smiles straight away.

'That's Yevgeny. You don't want to mess with this one, friend. My advice is to forget about it.'

'Ah, OK. No problem. He's dangerous, this Yevgeny?'

'He's inside, but I'd leave it alone if were you.'

'Hey, I'm here to party though, but, um, he's like a gangster, this Yevgeny?'

'Something like that. He's trouble for you if you're looking to…'

'No, no. You set me straight, boss.'

The guy has run out of patience, says to Travis, 'Keep moving in or go home, friend.'

He keeps moving to the counter, pays his $20 to get in.

Travis has the photo in his jacket pocket. If Yevgeny is here, he'd like the chance to show it to him. Get his reaction. He wanders inside down a tight hallway, then into the club proper. He is hit by a wall of sound through *Say So Snakehips Remix*. It is LOUD. The room is impossibly huge given its frontage. Travis can't believe it. He thinks Yevgeny will be in a private room. The big guy outside lost patience. He needs to find another source to Yevgeny. Is he a partying university undergraduate? Or a dangerous thug who picks up girls forcing them into a world of prostitution? He wants badly to find out. He wants to hurt someone after what happened to Paul and Katya. He doesn't give a shit who it is.

He sees him. Yevgeny, the neck tattoo, three small Chinese girls with him at a bar on the next level. A nasty looking thug next to him wearing an ushanka hat and a black t-shirt. Looking all around. Not part of the conversation. The man's huge arms and chest visible even from the floor below. Yevgeny's muscle. The bar doesn't look private. He wonders if the bouncer outside told someone what he said. Is there a camera on Travis right now? He goes to the bar closest to him, keeping his eyes on Yevgeny at all times. The music moves to *I don't care* by Justin Bieber. It's louder. He orders three Vodka shots. They come, he hits them one after the other, still looking up at the bar at the Russian Heir with his Asian girls and the big man in the hat. He thinks Yevgeny looks at him briefly before looking away.

He finds the staircase at one end of the bar, slowly climbs it to the other bar where they are. The four of them in the club but apart from everyone else.

He walks as close as he can up to Yevgeny. The big guy watches him come. Travis flashes his best smile, but the big Russian in the hat gives him nothing. He's about a metre-and-a-half from Yevgeny, smiles at him. Yevgeny smiles back.

Travis says loudly so he can be heard over the thumping music, 'Yevgeny, hi! My man!'

Yevgeny backs away from Travis. The big man in the hat doesn't move. Travis puts out his arms. Maybe Yevgeny recognises his face from somewhere, A few years ago Travis was on the front and back page of most Melbourne papers. Anyhow, he lets Travis come in, and Travis man hugs him, says, 'Hey, you remember me? I'm Travis Whyte. We partied way back at...'

'Yeah, yeah, I remember you man. How are you?'

'I'm good. Got to show you something.'

He reaches into the inside pocket of his jacket, takes out the photos from Facebook. The big guy still doesn't move. Travis puts the photos in Yevgeny's face, shouts, 'You know me, huh? You know these fucken girls to!? You know them?'

The big man in the hat starts to move, but he's slow. Travis lunges out, scrapes his right boot down his shin, hard as fuck. The big Russian screams in pain. Travis grazes down that shin again. The big man drops down on his haunches. Travis takes out the rubber sap, smashes it into the big man's knees and elbows, hard, vicious blows. The big man crumbles. Travis strikes him across the back of his head with the sap. Smashes it into his nose. The big Russian is crippled. Travis breaks his nose with another blow. Yevgeny looks on, shocked, as the big man screams. Travis grabs Yevgeny at the throat, says, 'You fucken know me now, man? Where are those girls? Where are they?'

He headbutts Yevgeny, hitting also his right eye.

Yevgeny is spooked. He's scared. His man taken out by this guy.

He knows about the girls.

He knows about the girls.

'Where are they?' Travis screams, smashing his elbow into Yevgeny's face, smashing the sap across his elbow, grabs his hair, drags him away, keeps dragging him down the stairs. Travis looking for an exit. If he can get him outside. He drags him down the hall towards the toilets, sees one at the end of the hall, probably alarmed. Bass music pumps louder and louder as Travis drags Yevgeny through the club. He sees the big bouncer from outside coming at him and drags the Russian Heir to the exit. He makes it to the door. Cracks the bar in the middle of the door and it opens. He burst out into a laneway. Still, he has Yevgeny, who is bleeding from that eye now in bad pain. He's not a fighter, even though he might look one. This is not his game. He's the seducer, not the enforcer. Travis shoves him onto the ground in the dirty laneway, smacks the sap across his back and legs, slams the emergency exit door shut. He unlocks the wheels on a big bin and drags it across the exit. Puts the locks back on front and back.

'Where are they? Where are the girls? You're on your own here. I'll fucken kill you, OK. Where are they?' He yells again, dragging him by his ponytail, kicking him in the face. Smashing the sap across a knee.

'Where are they?'

'I'll take you. I'll take you.'

Travis knows he has seconds. They're going to come bursting down the lane or out of the door any second. He hears them trying to force the doors against the big steel bin. He smashes Yevgeny in the stomach with the sap, once, twice, again and again. Hits him in the mouth, breaks a few teeth.

'Where are they? The address. The address.'

Yevgeny gives it to him. Travis swings the sap across the Russian's back and runs, runs fast down the laneway. He runs down to Elizabeth Street waiting behind another big garbage bin on wheels. Seconds later, two bouncers burst out of the emergency exit forcing their way past the huge bin. Two more come running down the laneway from the Swanston Street end. Travis sits, waits. The men look around. They can't leave Yevgeny or the club. They have work to do. He needs a doctor. They help him inside. Travis calls Detective Lois Baldock, gives her the address.

'Ring me if they're safe. Please, ring me if they're safe.'

'Where are you? What happened?'

Travis doesn't reply. He ends the call, waiting in a doorway on Elizabeth Street getting his breath back. It takes a few minutes until he's fine. No-one laid a finger on him. He surprised the shit out of them. He was lucky. He waits in the doorway some more, then walks along Elizabeth Street to Flinders Street. Walks back past the railway station, in dark now, the last train gone. He turns onto Swanston Street, goes into McDonalds, orders two cheeseburgers, large fries, a vanilla thick shake and takes it all to a seat facing the street. He eats hungrily. He wants to be in the city, close to Yevgeny, when the girls are found or not. If he was lying, he doesn't know what he'll do. He finishes his meal, orders a coffee, goes back to the seat at the window and waits and waits. Nearly two hours go by, and he starts to doubt himself. Doubt he did the wrong thing.

Baldock calls him.

'They found the girls. Outside. No-one in the house. The girls said a man took them from their room. Told them to get out and then disappeared.'

They had not been harmed, but both of them told the police they were held against their will, had been forced to work some shifts, that they were going to be taken somewhere interstate or overseas. It was enough for Travis to know they were held against their will, forced to work as prostitutes, that charges would be laid against Yevgeny. He called Jenny's father. He had already spoken to her. They would be home soon. He thanked Travis. He had found them, and this time he wasn't too late. He sat and looked out at the passing parade, got himself another coffee.

Things have been strange; Travis feels like a character in a book. Perry walks past the window. Travis feels his heart start beating out of control. He stares at Perry, but Perry looks straight ahead. Travis is frozen but can't breathe now, another panic attack starting. He gulps for air, sees him, dressed in bone-coloured chinos, a blue and white check shirt, a dark blue bomber jacket. Mr Ordinary, Dylan. It's him. The man who slashed Ann to pieces. Travis can barely stand. Perry and Dylan continue on.

Travis gets down on his knees. A security guard comes towards him, signals to his workmate, they both kneel down next to Travis.

'What's wrong, mate?' One of them asks.

'Can't breathe, I... I'll be alright... I.'

They lift him up, each taking an arm. Travis starts to feel a little better, but his heart is still beating hard. The guys walk him outside. Travis gets a deep breath into his lungs, shrugs the security guards off, runs, bent over, back towards Flinders Lane where Perry and Dylan headed to The Tunnel as planned.

He sees them when he is ten metres away. They have joined the line. Dylan puts his forearm on Perry's shoulder. Perry turns and smiles at him. Ann. Paul. Katya. Travis wants to kill them both. They progress in the queue. He can't get back in, no way. They edge further forward, Travis walks as close as he dares, yells out as loud as he can, 'Perry! Perry!'

Perry and Dylan turn, they both see Travis instantaneously. Perry smiles a thin smile. Dylan looks at him, expressionless, then it clicks with Perry who it is. Travis moves for them, but they split fast. Perry runs towards Elizabeth Street; Dylan bursts away from the queue zig-zagging through people away from Travis back to Swanston Street.

Travis follows Dylan. They're both on Swanston Street. Travis has him clear in his vision. Dylan doesn't look back, keeps running, Travis has him. He's cruising — he can run like this all night — but he's got to pick his moment to tackle him, to hurt him.

Dylan runs past Federation Square increasing his speed as he crosses over Princess Bridge. Travis runs faster too. This is it, he thinks. Dylan is making his break for it now. Travis accelerates, pumping his legs and arms. Dylan runs down a path to his left. Leading to the Yarra River, to boatsheds and grassy banks. He turns left back under Princess Bridge. Travis follows him. Dylan stops and turns. Travis wonders if there is CCTV under here. He doubts it.

Dylan says nothing, only stands there, smiling.

'What now, cunt?' Travis says.

Dylan takes a knife from the inside pocket of his bomber jacket and says, 'This is what. Come and get it. You hate me, don't you? You want to kill me. Come and get it.'

Travis takes his jacket off, wraps it around his left hand and lower arm. In jeans and a t-shirt only now. The sap in his right hand. He moves forward towards Dylan who backs away. Travis dives at him full pace, hitting Dylan in the chest. Dylan swings the blade as he crashes to the ground, cuts Travis above the top of his left eye. They both crash to the ground. Dylan gets up first, backs further away towards the damp grass embankment. Travis wipes the blood from above his eye with his jacket. Dylan says, 'That's the first cut. You remember Ann. You remember when you first saw her?'

Travis runs, dives at him again, knocking him to the ground. Dylan is lithe. He isn't strong. Travis isn't an unsuspecting young girl or a drugged boy. The blade drops out of Dylan's hand when he hits the turf, he reaches for it, but Travis has it in an instant. Dylan tries to roll away, Travis smashes the sap across his nose, then has him by the throat of his stupid Country Road checked shirt. This little rich boy. That's what Travis sees. A spoilt rich boy. He couldn't be anything else, dressed like that. So plain he's almost invisible. Travis drops the sap.

'Why'd you do it?' Travis asks. 'Why'd you kill her?'

Dylan looks at him, gives him a little half-smirk, says, 'I was bored.'

Travis shivs him right under the right rib cage, buries the knife in him deep. Sees the shock, then slowly the light go out in Dylan's eyes. He leaves it in there staring at him, then slowly pulls it out. Dylan slides down the small grass embankment helped by Travis as he watches him sway in the water at the edge of the embankment. He pushes Dylan with his boots, sends him out into the current and it slowly drags him away from Travis in the direction of the estuary.

Travis walks away. Walks up to the Rowing sheds, finds a seat, sits down. He calls Lois Baldock for the second time that night. She answers. He says, 'I killed someone in self-defence. I believe him to be the killer of Ann Gables at the Cross Motel in Kings Cross.'

'What the fuck are you playing at, Travis?'

'What I told you. I killed the killer of Ann Gables in self-defence. He came at me with a knife. His body is floating down the Yarra towards the estuary.'

'Where are you?'

'I'm at the boatshed closest to Princess Bridge.'

'Don't move.'

'No, ma'am.'

Travis stands up, lights a cigarette. Thinks of Ann Gables, Paul, his old friend, Katya. All because he was bored. That's it, that's what he said.

'*I was bored.*'

CHAPTER FORTY-THREE

The police found the body further along the embankment. It had been stopped by a big metal sieve that normally collected cans and plastic bottles. It took Angelo ten hours to get there. Travis slept well for a killer. He and Angelo sat side by side across the table from Lois Baldock and another detective. Baldock identifies herself and flicks the IC recorder on.

Angelo says, 'My client won't be saying anything further. He gave a brief description of what happened to this deceased person. He will willingly have a DNA test. There is no body at present, is that correct?'

'No, we have a body,' Baldock says, smirks at both of them, saying, 'You think you have this down cold, don't you counsellor? No witness, no CCTV, self-defence plea, missing person in the form of a pimp-dealer from Sydney named Perry, who was supposedly working with the deceased in planning the unsolved murder of Ann Gables. That about it?'

'My client won't be saying anything further.'

'What if the DNA test finds links to the deceased?'

'He acted in self-defence. This man killed two young women and a teenage boy. My client is not obliged to answer any further questions.'

'Interview over,' Baldock says, nodding her head at Travis, who nods slowly back at her.

Angelo and Travis are in an Uber heading for the airport. Angelo says, 'I went through the books that Ahn managed to get from the safe at The Angel, found more than enough proof that Billy was co-owner of the club with your friend, Farez.'

'Ahn now gets what?'

'Farez has agreed for Ahn to be recognised as the co-owner of the club, for her to be a silent partner. Ahn has agreed to the fifty-percent deal but won't be silent.'

'No, I'm sure she won't.'

'Mr Chui wants to put you on a retainer.'

'Doing what?'

'Whatever comes up. Suffice to say you won't be working in any of his gambling clubs, not as a doorman, I wouldn't think. It will be around sixty K a year plus bonuses, etc.'

'Can you do up a contract between me and Chui?'

'I can, but...'

'But, I'm still going to carry on with my own business using my private enquiry agent license. You'll have to include something about that in the contract. I think I proved I can do two things at once, play football, and generally be a pain the arse.'

'Agreed.'

The Uber drops them off at Tullamarine. Travis finds a quiet spot and rings Babus.

'Travis, hi, I'm glad you're alright. Ahn has been telling me about what you went through and...'

'Did you call her, or did she call you?'

'She called me, why?'

'I'm curious, and yeah, been a big few days, a big few weeks. Never be anything like them again, I reckon.'

'Knowing you, Travis, I don't think that's a safe bet.'

'I miss you, everything about you.'

'That's sweet, Travis. I miss you too.'

A long pause.

Babus asks him, 'Did they find that guy? The one who sent the killer to the motel you worked in where the girl died. I think Ahn said his name was...'

'Perry. No, they didn't find him. CCTV lost him when he got in what they think was an Uber. They couldn't get the make or plates on the car.'

"Does that bother you?'

'It hurts me, but I'm going to be trying as hard as I can to get him. This thing isn't finished, not yet.'

They promise to see each soon.

Travis ends the call.

He wonders about Olsen. Is he corrupt or not?

He thinks about his father.

He has a story to tell him.

The End

Dear reader,

We hope you enjoyed reading *Going All The Way*. Please take a moment to leave a review, even if it's a short one. Your opinion is important to us.

Discover more books by Sean O'Leary at https://www.nextchapter.pub/authors/sean-oleary

Want to know when one of our books is free or discounted? Join the newsletter at http://eepurl.com/bqqB3H

Best regards,
Sean O'Leary and the Next Chapter Team

ABOUT THE AUTHOR

Sean O'Leary is a writer from Melbourne, Australia. He has published two literary short story collections 'My Town' and 'Walking.' A collection of crime stories called 'Wonderland.' Also close to forty short stories in small and large press all over the world. His novella 'Drifting' was the winner of the Great Novella Search. He has published two crime novellas 'The Heat' and 'Preston Noir.' He likes to walk all over the face of the earth, travel a lot, supports Melbourne Football Club (a life sentence), and writes like a demon.

CPSIA information can be obtained
at www.ICGtesting.com
Printed in the USA
BVHW071046041121
620779BV00005B/72

9 781006 398254